Latte for Leyla

Latte for Leyla

MELANIE GREENE

First edition: March 2022

Latte for Leyla/by Melanie Greene

ISBN: 978-1-941967-35-5

David!
Sweet lucky number 13, this one is all yours

Chapter One

The first time Leyla Robinson heard about that spring's Keep Surfside Swell Expo was at the weekly beach bonfire.

She'd taken her short board, Rainbow, out to catch some sunset waves, and noticed the group gathered around their usual fire pit as she came up out of the water. Laughter, chat, shared coolers and blankets as the Pacific crashed into dusk.

Her besties Sally and Noah insisted she was more than welcome at the Friday night bonfires, and it was true that people made room for her when she showed up. Even if she did basically just sit there with less than half an idea of what to say once she and Noah, who owned her favorite surf shop, had caught up on surfing, and she and Sally, who was an academic librarian, traded whatever gossip they had from the world up on campus.

Okay: Sally told her the gossip. Leyla rarely had any.

What Leyla had was a routine. She had class hours, and lab hours, and work hours, and surfing on Surfside's best beach.

That was her grind, day in and day out, and had been for years. And maybe—only maybe—she was wrestling with the tiniest of undercurrents about the impending end of her academic career. She was quietly mulling that over in her gentle post-surf euphoria when a conversation caught her attention.

Mateo, who'd recently taken over a seat on the city council, was explaining his latest initiative. "It's an Expo to feature Surfside's locally owned businesses and highlight the community. All I want is for someone at the university to return my calls, point me in the right direction to see if we can get them invested in promoting it somehow."

Sally was shaking her head. "And this is why I shouldn't have spent so long burning bridges in my quest to stay out of university politics. I know of a few associate deans who could get you to the right spot, but not one of them will do me a favor these days. And it's nothing against your Expo plans, because I'm sure those are great and worthwhile. Let me think about it, though. I'm sure I can come up with someone who wouldn't say no the second I walk through the door."

Mateo dropped his head. "Ugh, sorry. I was mostly venting. I didn't bring it up to pressure you."

Noah laughed. "You are a terrible politician. You're supposed to leap on her offer to help."

It was thoroughly outside of Leyla's character for her to interrupt everyone's chorus of joking advice about how Mateo could be a more ruthless mover-and-shaker, to say, "I think I can help."

Sally gave her a look like, "Girl, why is your mouth open? Let somebody else fight this fight." She just shrugged at her friend because, honestly, did Sally really think that she would, for once, not add something else to her plate?

Even though—and the realization was burrowing deep into her chest like a clam into the sand at low tide—helping Mateo meant eradicating a line she'd managed to hold firm throughout her years in Surfside.

Because thing was, as soon as Mateo and Sally discussed the problem, she'd put together a few pieces of info and come up with a potential solution. It meant dealing with the associate dean who'd been her undergrad thesis advisor and was now an inescapable part of her Masters in Coastal Science and Policy. Dean Tyler was a skilled networker, which meant he was invaluable to grad students like her who relied on his connections. But it also meant his constant schemes to increase his own social capital.

So, if she went to him on Keep Surfside Swell's behest, presenting it as a chance to strengthen his own ties with the city government, and maybe impress others within the university administration, she thought he would go for that. But he would also seize the chance to call this an exchange of favors, and she knew as well as Sally did what the quid for his quo would be.

Dean Tyler wasn't subtle. He wanted the School of Earth and Marine Sciences to be perceived as diverse, no matter the actual, slowly changing, demographics. And instead of working on better pathways to encourage a more representative base of incoming scientists, like she'd suggested more than once, he wanted to make Leyla the face of the program.

She'd spent years edging past his suggestion, aiming a bright smile and long list of research obligations his way whenever she sensed the subject weighing down the air between them. She didn't mind her pic accompanying her academic work, or any kind of candids that represented reality. She minded being used to fabricate a story the university hadn't yet earned.

Sally was still eyeing her skeptically.

Leyla wrinkled her nose at her friend. "It'll be what it is. Besides, it's been almost seven years without my bright diverse self appearing in a single brochure. That's gotta be some kind of record."

They'd been friends since Leyla's freshman year, so Sally knew Leyla's flaws nearly as well as Leyla did herself. Not least among them was her drive to charge forward and fix things as soon as she saw a need she could fulfill. Some ex once sent her a meditation about not saying yes to everything that was asked of her. It was seriously the last straw proving that she was in the wrong relationship.

"If he thinks I'm going around saying yes when I mean no, he can't grip the slightest of nuances about me," she'd told Sally. Looking back, that was one of their first long chats that solidified their friendship. "I'm constantly saying no when people ask things of me. Hell, I turned down like nineteen attempts to recruit me for free labor before I even got to my first set of midterms up here. It's the things no one asks of me that I'm too prone to volunteer for."

Sally had snorted in understanding and offered the first of many high fives that would punctuate their friendship. She'd also offered up advice from her perspective as another Black woman in academia, including to be thoughtful about how others might approach her to improve their own optics. Which explained the raised eyebrows look the librarian was shooting at her now.

She shrugged back at her. In truth, she never expected to get this close to the end of her academic career without having to give in once too often when someone wanted her on a poster or panel or paper with no regard to her own interest in the subject. And not incidentally, to feel free to downplay her many solid and impressive achievements as just another diversity checkmark for the institution.

Which is why she spent so long determining exactly which opportunities were the ones to aim for as she built the career of her dreams. Was co-authoring a paper on hiking and camping trails on the alluvial plains going to help her save the oceans and get her the job offer she wanted? No, so why would she devote her time, her brain, and her lovely face to the effort, when instead she could accept the invite to speak on a panel about establishing regulatory best practices for tide pool tourists.

The lingering skepticism on Sally's face was probably because persuading the university to play nice with the Keep Surfside Swell Expo wouldn't help drop Leyla's dream job in her lap. But her resume was already a beauty of bullet-pointed perfection. Every move she and her advisors could come up with, she'd already made.

Now it was a long slog of applications and interviews and the need to destress while attempting to outmaneuver her Machiavellian academic rival, Chad.

She may as well get that relief by helping her friends and this community she'd come to value so dear.

And it wasn't like Mateo and his partner Alicia would be hard work with. She'd liaise a bit with them, let Dean Tyler get up in her business with his entirely unhidden agenda, and everyone would be happy.

Easy as cutting into a corduroy swell during a daybreak tide with an offshore breeze.

Leyla was at bonfire.

Someone coulda fucking warned him, but no.

Austin Wells halted just outside the ring of lights and worked to get his face under control. His cousin Noah flashed him a Shaka sign, all casual and harmless, like he hadn't broken his promise to give Austin a heads-up if Leyla showed.

He had laughed his fucking head off at Austin's ongoing need to practice how to talk to her without gibbering, even after all this time knowing her. But he had promised.

Yet there she sat next to his sister Alicia. Casual, but, to Austin, not even a little harmless as she sprawled on a serape, t-shirt slapping loosely over the pulled down top half of her wetsuit. Her surfboard was propped just far enough from the cluster of people that only the flames bouncing glimmery reflections off its yellow stripes alerted him. It was like the dimmest reflection of Leyla's own brightness, which nothing outshone.

As always, she was magic. A magnet, collecting every micron of the steel he tried to sneak into his weak-ass bones. But every bit of his mettle flew out of him and collected around her, adding to her value even as he stumbled to stand up without the help of his bones.

So, yeah, he was a fucking disaster area, head to toe. A jellyfish instead of a spine. Hearts surely flying out of his eyes. Ears as useless as when he was standing over the machine frothing the hazelnut creamer she liked in her lattes. Pulse triple-timing like he'd downed three triple espressos in as many minutes.

She was so perfect. How the fuck was he always so ruined by sitting within ten feet of her? And not to put too fine a point on it, how the fuck was he coming off just then, sitting all glazed and probably drooling. Unable to hear what anyone was saying, to see anyone but her, or act in any way like he had a single spark of chill tucked deep within his soul.

Something cold hit his leg and he jumped. Noah had lobbed a beer his way, surely knowing he wasn't paying enough attention to catch it. His grin proved how unrepentant he was about how frothy the drink would now be.

"Heard you got that elevator install scheduled," his cousin said, which at least was a topic Austin could discuss without going up in embarrassed flames. So one point for Noah.

He nodded with begrudging gratitude, slurped the head off the beer, and launched into a description of the project they'd undertaken to increase accessibility for their auxiliary business.

Alicia and Mateo asked her to drop by Pier Three when she was done surfing, saying they'd be upstairs in the conference suite all morning working on their plans.

While spraying Rainbow down with the grey water hose, and stashing her in the rack set along the side of the coffee shop, she spied Austin working through the walk-up order window. By the time she'd snagged her bag from the storage cubbies mounted next to the rack, he'd disappeared, but a hazelnut latte sat on the pick-up counter, labeled for her in Austin's familiar scrawl. She offered payment to the barista still at work, but Ruthie waved her off.

She'd never been up to the Pier Three Studios and Conference Suite, but between Sally's and Noah's various comments, she'd garnered several details of how it came into being. The Wells siblings—Abraham, Alicia, and Austin—had needed to juice their income to afford the building their coffee shop inhabited. So, Alicia moved out of the upstairs studio apartment and the siblings converted it into a couple of recording studios and a quieter meeting space than customers to the coffee shop downstairs would find.

Alicia caught her looking around while Mateo distributed paperwork around the conference table. "It's great, isn't it?"

It looked like office spaces tended to look. Table, cabinets, a couple of counters. Current, she supposed, with fresh paint and all that. It wasn't really her milieu to judge, but Alicia's face was expectant, so she nodded.

"Comfortable chairs," she offered.

They arranged themselves with Alicia at the head of the table. "Aren't they? One of Austin's buddies hooked him up from a place that was downsizing. He found the table through some other guy."

"Whenever you need anything," Mateo said, "look to Austin. He always knows a guy."

She took a noncommittal slip of her latte, because when would she need a guy? She lived in grad student housing, and would go from there to living on boats a bunch of the time, if everything lined up like she hoped. She'd find some generic kind of rental for the land-based half of her life.

"He did all the design and labor up here, too," went on Alicia, who was laying the sales pitch on a little thick.

She extracted her notebook and pulled forward the papers, determined to put them all back on track.

It wasn't long before she got to the agenda behind all of Alicia's praise of her flaky baby brother. Because the thing was, Austin was cute as fuck, sure, but that didn't mean he was anything other than a flake. Leyla was sure he has plenty of redeeming qualities, building interiors apparently one of them, but he also, no matter what the others tried to paint as positives, spent so much time scattered and skittering every time she saw him, that she was plenty comfortable with her opinion of him.

And comfortable with whatever face she made when Alicia said, "We're going to leave all this in you and Austin's hands, since we've committed our time to navigating everything for the vendors."

Mateo winced when he clocked her visible skepticism. "You'll be surprised," he said, all reassuring and hopeful.

Leyla was pulling all the paperwork together, and didn't quite manage a nod. Their promise of surprise notwithstanding, she could handle this project on her own. It had clear goals, and she was already coming up with plans.

No need to make her life harder by involving Austin in the process.

That furrowed crease above Alicia's eyes wasn't gonna sway her. Nerves of steel, that's what Leyla had on offer. And that meant she'd find a way to talk Dean Tyler into championing this Expo with the Regents, submit to whatever performative nonsense was required of her, copy Austin on a few email updates, and emerge afterward with a happy Dean, a delighted community, and another completed task in the rear view of her road paved with successes.

"Heads up, here comes your girl," Ruthie had said, but Austin was already making up her drink. His position behind the La Marzocco offered him a clear and tantalizing glimpse of the surf-misted halo of Leyla's hair as she racked her board against the beach-facing wall of his shop.

"I should have known," Ruthie grinned, shaking her head as Austin dashed cocoa and cinnamon on top of the foam and set the latte where Leyla would look for it. "You could wait for her to ask for that, you know. Maybe she'd like something else for a change."

Austin shot her a quelling look.

"All I'm saying is, you take her order, that gets the two of you talking. Maybe only about a dozen words each, but hey, the first dozen are the hardest."

Austin didn't bother to answer. The door was opening. He slid his Pier Three apron over his head, hanging it on the wall hook and disappearing into the tiny back office. If he switched on the radio fast enough, he wouldn't hear the slap of Leyla's flip-flops across the floor, much less her lilt of a voice laughing at whatever jokes Ruthie opted for to torment him.

Austin didn't have time for laughs that were pure sunshine. He was figuring out shifts for the next month, now that Cleo needed different hours. Had he needed to retreat just at that second to work on the schedule? No. But even his strongest Sumatran dark roast was useless against the beacon of Leyla's sunscreen and salt waves scent, and one glimpse of her strong legs or the toenails she always painted to match the ocean would derail him from any kind of ordered thinking.

So he didn't think about her. Not at all. Not one moment of the entire time she spent in the room just above his head.

Once he heard the rattle of the treads on the stairs down from the conference room, indicating Leyla's departure, he popped out to ask Ruthie what she'd meant by writing "newd foists" in the "What can we do to make your work feel better?" box he'd added to the timekeeping software.

He found his sister and Mateo and Ruthie all standing around smirking at him like they knew secrets at his expense.

He wasn't interested in their nonsense. Not when he could retreat to the office and shove Abraham's paperwork aside, making room to sit on the desk. On one side, he set his tablet, open to the employee comments. On the other, his legal pad with all the notes he'd jotted down about work schedules. He snagged his pads of sticky notes off the windowsill and started transferring the information. Every employee got their own color. Morning shifts on the top half of the window, afternoons on the bottom, and yes, he would input it all in the computer later, and yes, it would be just as color coded and should be just as easy for him to shift around digitally, but he didn't care.

He needed his pens and paper and window system.

It worked for him, and it wasn't in anyone's interests to try to make him do something different.

Chapter Three

Yuji was always good for covering the counter by himself in a pinch. Especially since Austin timed his arrival to coincide with the mid-morning lull.

In no way was he paying heed to Alicia's protests as he snagged her by the wrist and dragged her out the back for a conversation.

"What the actual fuck?" Alicia played innocent, but he saw her eyes shifting around.

"Ha. You know what."

"What do I know?"

"You don't even have the grace to tell me yourself. You made your boyfriend do the dirty work."

"Maybe I just wanted to spare myself the way you'd moan and gripe about it, when you know as well as I do how important the Expo is. If we don't get the university on board ..."

"Obviously. You don't have to tell me things I already know. What you do have to tell me is why the hell you're getting me involved. There's no point to it, Licie. I'm hardly the one with any sway at the university. Plus, it's not like Leyla has any kind of use for me. It's bullshit for you to force her to deal with me."

"I'm not forcing her. She can say no as well as anybody else in the world. Maybe better than. That woman knows her own mind."

"Did you ask her or did you just lay it on her? Did you assume she'd be totally fine with it instead of giving her a choice?"

Alicia crossed her arms. "If she wanted to say no—"

"She wouldn't say no to you. She's too nice. Especially with you and Mateo sitting there with your please-help-us eyes, acting like the fate of the universe depends on her agreement. You know she'd never say no to that."

He was lying to himself. He was lying to his sister. Leyla would say no to anything she wanted to say no to. If she's ever been susceptible to that kind of polite pressure to conform, she'd stamped it out of herself by the time she got to this point in her life: nearly done with her master's degree and ready to save the entire damn planet via the strength of her will alone.

But his wrong statements weren't the point.

Point was, Leyla was a generous, sweet, brilliant, dedicated, perfect woman, and she cared about their community and goals of the Surfside Swell campaign. So even if it meant being stuck with him as a partner, she'd bear with the task. Even though nobody should be pressured to deal with him.

"She's fine with it," Alicia said, like that was the issue.

"Well, good, but maybe I'm not fine with it. You're sneaking around, making some kind of ploy like she needs me, when you know damn well she doesn't need me. This is all some weird scheme of yours that doesn't make any sense, and you need to stop."

His breath was labored, which only pissed him off more. He was so bent out of shape he could have winkled into the awkward narrow gap between the building's wall and staircase, and finally retrieved that hex key he'd dropped a few months back while tightening the rivets on one of the stair treads.

Yeah, it was just a hex key, and he owned a half dozen of the same gauge, but it ate at him that he hadn't yet managed to get it back.

Like his sister loved pointing out how different they were, Alicia stood solid and straight and strong. Like she gained steadiness by throwing him for a loop.

He knew what she was up to. "I'm on to you," he said. "And I don't like it."

"If you don't have time to work on this, I can ask Quinn or someone put out the call."

He scoffed and turned away, grabbing the coat hanger he'd glued a magnet to and stashed by the dumpster. Maybe a sharper curve would work to snag the hex key, so he could slide it to within reach.

"I can't just tell her I'm not going to work with her. Not after you've already exploded your fancy bombshell." He wasn't gonna say it to his siblings, but lord knew Leyla didn't need any more reasons to think him a squirrelly, useless excuse of a man.

The magnet clacked against something, but when he retracted it a few centimeters, nothing dragged along with it. He lowered his shoulder and set the wire tapping gently around the concrete again. Alicia sank onto the steps, so he could only catch her in his line of sight if he made it a point to look for her. Not that he was making it a point.

She crossed her arms. "You're telling me in one breath that she can't say no to helping, and in the next that she volunteered because she wants to help. And a second later you're mad that we need help at all, that we're imposing on you. And now you're refusing to take the out I'm offering. You're not making any sense, Austin."

The magnet clacked again something again. This time

when he pulled cautiously back, he heard the scrape of steel, meaning his fishing expedition had netted him his hex key. He closed his eyes, because for whatever reason it was easier to concentrate on reeling the wire hanger back towards him if his eyes were closed.

Also because he didn't need to see his sister's impatient pose in his periphery while she accused him of the inability to think the way she thought he should think. He didn't need to see her laser glare to know her opinion of his flighty brainpower.

His hex key scraped another little way towards him. He imagined he might even be able to see it if he opened his eyes, but he didn't.

The rasp of the handle and slight creak of door hinges he should oil meant Yuji's approach. He called for Alicia with just enough need under his voice that they both caught his warning of an influx of customers

"Yeah," Alicia said. He heard her take a step down before she asked, "Austin?"

He turned his head and opened his eyes.

She dropped her arms but didn't make any gesture like she was actually sorry for what she'd done to him.

He looked back towards the gap between the wall and the stairs. "Go."

Closing his eyes, he held still until the shutting door meant he was alone.

Another centimeter. Another. It was nearly out. His shoulder was burning and he was holding his breath, but the key was sliding closer. He fed the wire back towards his chest, just another centimeter. The steady scrape-scrape hitched as the wrench hit some kind of obstruction. Maybe a little seam in the concrete.

He cracked open one eye and peered into the space. He got nothing, so he wrinkled the wire to check if the magnet was as solid on the tool as he could make it, and resumed his tedious reeling in. There was a low glint in the darkness under the stairs, and he was staring at it so closely that he didn't notice at first that the wire was too light and buoyant under his fingers.

The tantalizing glint hadn't moved any closer.

He tapped the coat hanger and the wire tinged back at him, lacking any of its former tensile strength. Austin let his head plop to the pavement and withdrew the coat hanger. The magnet had fallen off. All that remained was a blob of epoxy, so now his once-clever retrieval gadget was just an awkwardly bent wire, and his tool remained too far away to be of any use.

Chapter Four

"No, you're the one who's got it twisted," Sally said, cutting off Leyla's teasing accusation of misunderstanding someone's nonsense in their group chat.

They looked at each other and doubled over laughing. Luckily the day was over, and Sally's coworkers had left, or they'd have gotten that 'Be quiet in the library' look from Derek, the new, took-his-job-too-seriously, Loan Services intern.

He hadn't been all that sanguine about letting Leyla stay inside when Sally locked the doors behind him, come to that. But Sally just wrinkled her nose at him and reminded him that adversity was good for the soul. His expression also made them cackle with un-library-like glee, but neither cared.

Sally wiped her eyes and waved away the reference to one of their inside jokes. "I don't know why you are so determined to do this. I'm as addicted to Pier Three's coffee as the next person, but—"

"It's not for the coffee shop. All that crisis of theirs has been sorted out, far as I can make out." She could have just asked someone for the details. But instead, she did her usual thing of listening from the periphery and piecing together info. If it was to do with her degree, she was always ready to get full-on investigative and question everything. But for what passed as her social life, Leyla never knew how to interrupt everyone else's flow to seek clarity. That's why her volunteering for this Expo thing to start with still had her surprised at herself. Helping the community, yes, that was on brand. It was speaking up in a crowd to volunteer that normally dried up all her intentions.

Sally nodded to confirm that Pier Three had survived their earlier troubles. "Thanks to your boy Austin."

"He is not my boy. That child is no more my boy than he is everybody else's boy. Have you ever seen him not flirt? I swear I saw him making those puppy dog eyes at a seagull once."

Sally snorted. "What'd the seagull do?"

"Settled down and hopped closer, of course. Same as everybody else he peeps with those ..." Leyla cut herself off, because what Austin did with his powerful eyes was hardly the point. "Anyway, maybe it was the Pier Three people who're putting this Expo together, but weren't you the one that gave them the idea in the first place?"

Sally's smirk was impish. "All I did is mentioned how there used to be a community festival. They're the ones that ran with it."

"Uh huh. And did you or did you not also mention that they used to run campus shuttles to the festival for free and that the university passed out flyers during Family Weekend?"

Sally waved that off, too, because Leyla wasn't the only Black woman in academia in their twosome. She knew how to maintain her distance from anything that might importune her as well as Leyla did. It was Sally's using knowledge to act in self-preservation that led to her burnt bridges with Dean

Tyler. And with a couple of others in the administration who were equally determined to remain butthurt when she imposed the same limits on her availability and visibility as did her peers and predecessor.

They both knew well what kind of machinations Dean Tyler would get up to, once Leyla approached him for help with the Surfside Swell Expo. None of it would surprise her. "The main thing is that I find a way to do this without Chad finding out. Once he decides that I'm quote using my demographics unquote to get ahead, he will never let it go."

"Hasn't he already decided that's the truth? What's it matter what he thinks?"

"There's a difference between him deciding it, and him having something he can produce as supposed proof for the people at Dunlavy. He's been pouring his poison about this since we got our internships, and now that Trisha got hired away to the feds, the ground is fertile for more of his bullshit."

Trisha had been their direct supervisor during the summer internship, and the only person who'd pushed back against Chad's 'I must be the best intern ever since everyone else got here on affirmative action' narrative. It wasn't like Chad hadn't also earned the internship spot, but it rankled that she'd gotten fully glowing reviews throughout, while he'd messed up a data set so badly everyone had to pull extra hours bringing it back to the beginning to start over. Yet he was as in-contention for the permanent position as she was. "I'm not about letting his poisoned bullshit ruin my chance of getting the Dunlavy job."

Sally offered some of her salt and vinegar chips. "I think you're mixing up some metaphors there, friend. Either he poisoning the soil, or it's fertile, or it needs manure. You kind of got to pick one."

"Psh. I've got to do no such thing. Only thing I've got to

do is figure out how to pose for a series of photos of multicultural life on campus without Chad knowing."

Sally pursed her lips.

"What? You have an idea?"

Her friend slid over to her computer and clicked around. "This came across the server yesterday. I don't know if it is something you can do without Chad knowing, but I'm thinking if you maybe go to Tyler and drop it in the conversation?" She swiveled the screen to Leyla.

Creasing her brow, Leyla scanned the posting about a committee to review the university's diversity action plan. "Oh, hell yeah. I would far rather tell them how to assemble a focus group than get paraded around at a bullshit networking event. Okay, send that to me?"

Sally nodded.

"Thanks. Now. What do I say to Tyler so he keeps it under wraps, but still helps with the Surfside Swell Expo?"

A couple of hours later, she packed up the remains of the meal she'd carried into the library past Derek's disapproving frown, along with the notepads they'd been using and everything Sally had printed from the archives about the university's connection to the community.

They'd highlighted various bits of language about valuing the individual character of Surfside, and how honoring the town's legacy of independence helped mold scholars with the determination to bring their vibrant, sustainable visions to everywhere the world took them after leaving the hallowed halls of the university.

A lot of it was PR nonsense, but PR nonsense was what made donors happy.

"Okay, you're the best and wisest friend on earth," she said, hugging Sally.

"Tell me something I don't know. Now, go away before Derek shows up to report you for after-hours activities."

Before she backed out the door, she swiveled to call Sally out on the way she kept lingering on the new guy's emotional state. "Speaking of getting it twisted ..." And she ran off to the shuttle lot before she could hear the substance of Sally's indignant response.

Chapter Five

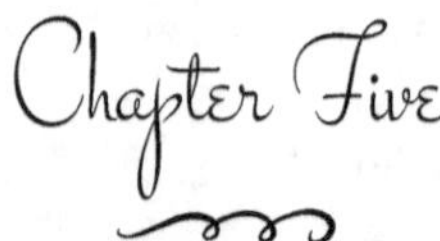

Austin packed away his tools and lined them up along his hallway. Was it a pain in the ass, living with his bathroom all torn up? Yep. But did it mean ending his workday was like two hundred percent easier? Also, yep.

When he was working on a tenant's space, he had to haul everything in and out every time, plus there was no leaving behind the ten or dozen things he might possibly need. Everything had to go with him, and no matter how his brother shook his head at Austin's supposed lack of organization, that meant keeping constant track of drills and shims, wrenches and bolts, snakes and ladders.

He sniggered and glanced at Abraham's bedroom door. His brother had gone off to visit his girlfriend and was missing out on all kinds of humor because of it. Shame for him. And when he got back, he was moving in with Callie. Alicia had already left the building their family owned to live with Mateo.

So, screw his lonely ass, seemed to be his siblings' new philosophy. Not that he wanted to live with the way they bought into Mom and Dad's whole, "Everybody look out for

Austin, cause he's too scattered and immature to take care of himself," thing that had comprised his whole fucking life.

Their folks had gone out of their way to ensure no one was infantilizing Abe, and it was like they thought the best way for Abe to know they weren't babying him was to treat Austin like the least capable person in the whole Wells clan. Sure, he was the youngest. And of course, Abraham having just the one arm didn't make him in the least incapable of navigating the world. But Austin's prefrontal cortex—yes, he knew science things—was as developed as the rest of his siblings, so maybe Dad and Mom could wrap their heads around treating him as such?

Which reminded him. He planted himself in front of his work wall. It was the surface above his dresser, which he'd painted with a high gloss magnetic paint and used to keep track of all his building maintenance shit. He moved a note about checking on his plumbing order to the urgent zone and gathered the notes for everything he'd done in 407 and 413. He re-read to assure himself he'd finished all the tasks and there wasn't anything more he needed to jot down. He wasn't going to charge 413 for installing their new cabinet knobs.

Everything looked right, so he clipped the notes to the magnet of things he would report to Dad as complete. He was checking the super email for any new tasks when the knock he'd been trying to forget about came.

Like any amount of hanging sheetrock could fool him into forgetting that Leyla Robinson was coming to his apartment.

He glanced around like somehow he'd unknowingly imported a mess to the kitchen and living room. Nope, they were still as tidy as he'd worked to make them. And there wasn't much to do about his personal untidiness. He surely had too much plaster dust in the hair, but there was nothing he could do about that. No time to go down to 104—his temporary bathroom while his was out of commission—and take a shower. Anyway, it hardly mattered what he looked like. Any given time Leyla saw him, he was in a wetsuit, a barista apron, a tool belt. Not one iteration of his attire could turn him into the kind of guy she'd be looking for. Assuming she was even looking.

She had way too much brilliance going on to make time for a college dropout whose only long-term jobs were with his family members.

"Leyla, hey yes, come in." Austin stopped talking, but kept that whole energetic thing go on. It always made her think he was wriggling his toes every time he tried to stand still. He flashed one of his abashed grins and scrubbed at the back of his head, which let fly some kind of explosion of dust or dandruff.

He clocked the way she was blinking at his dust halo and dragged his hand forward check it out, then quickly hopped over to the kitchen sink and started scrubbing. "Come in. Sorry. I've been hanging sheetrock in the bathroom."

"You remodeling? Did you get a pipe burst or something? Same thing happened to my sister last year; she kept sending me YouTube links of people doing repair jobs to ask if I thought it was worth her fixing it all up herself." And then she remembered all the bragging his sister had done. "Oh, hey, you probably make those YouTube videos your own self."

He rubbed a damp towel over his hair, leaving it all kinds of which way, and still not swiping away the line of dust on his neck. Looking like a baby bird of some kind didn't make him self-conscious enough to hold back his grins or dim the way his eyes shined at her.

"You want a drink? Snack? I've got some fruit salad I could dip up."

She tapped the water bottle in the mesh pocket of her messenger bag. "I'm all set. Don't worry, you can be off the clock."

He was nodding even though his grin went down a megawatt or two. "Yeah, no, it was hospitality, you know? You're my guest. Anyway, sit down." He tipped his chin towards the four-person dining set with most of its surface clear. "Or the sofa if you prefer?"

She slipped into one of the seats on the clear side of the table. "This is good."

Took him a sec to gather his drink and some papers from the sofa before he joined her. Enough time to note the table was solid and the surface smooth and dry, placing it above at least two-thirds of the variously wobbly or sticky tables in classrooms and field offices or cafes where she worked projects.

Not Pier Three's tables, she remembered, and wasn't that interesting. Seemed Mr. Maintenance kept things shipshape at work as well as at home.

Once he finally settled across from her, she passed over the hard copies of everything she'd worked out after talking to Sally. "I've roughed out the steps we'll take getting the university's cooperation in promoting Surfside Swells' Expo as the primary objective, with secondary goals of obtaining sponsorship and a commitment for ongoing participation. I broke down the objectives into likely tasks, then—" She reached over and flipped his packet to the next page. "I roughed out a timeline using the Expo dates as the end point and estimating how many hours each subtask will take. The next page is a preliminary task list so we can maybe assign a few of those things to you and you can let me know if there's anything I'm missing about the Expo that we should add to the presentation I'll make."

He flipped back to the first page and silently read from the top, twirling a ballpoint in his fingers like he was gotta go audition for drum line any second now. Soon as he tilted his head, she leaned in to see if she could figure out which part he was reading, in case he wanted her to expand on it. But his face didn't change as he flipped the page, and then the next, and then the next. After he finished skimming all the info she'd synthesized from the research she'd done with Sally, he sat back and dropped the pen, drumming his fingers against his jeans instead.

"You've got questions," she said, because you didn't spend as much time tutoring and TAing and training as she did without getting to know when people weren't following her.

As long as he didn't opt to mansplain her research back at her, she was fine with explaining anything he didn't get.

"Not about the timeframes at all, even though I will point out you never checked to see what ins I've got up on campus to help work out the big ask. But aside from letting me take on a few of the tasks, this looks like you've project managed an entire workflow only for yourself."

So, he understood project management. Good for him.

He reached for his pen, halting just before his fingers wrapped around the shaft, and shoved both hands under his thighs. "Leyla, if you ... you just don't know what use I am, that's one thing. We can talk that through. But I think what this means." He nodded at the paperwork and swallowed heavily, his Adam's apple bobbing. "I think you don't want to work with me at all. And I'm not about to force my company on you. We can set you up with somebody else, or let you go it alone. Whatever you need. I'm not—it's okay, if you feel like you can't spend time with me, specifically. I'm not gonna kick up a fuss about it. You can even just head out now until and, I'll, I don't know, text Mateo that I'm too busy with my remodel to do this. No one will question you finding someone else you'd rather work with."

Chapter Six

The actual fuck? He thought she was going to soothe his hurt baby-man feelings because she applied her genius to the task at hand? Nope, nah, no way.

She eyed him fidgeting across from her, and blushing. The boy was blushing? So maybe he noticed how he was showing his ass with his 'please pat me on the head and tell me I'm worthy' bullshit.

Know who told Leyla she was worthy? Leyla Robinson, that's who. She didn't have the time or luxury to go asking random men if they valued her. Not that she was interested in their opinions, which was clearly not something that Austin Wells could say.

Well, let him work out his neediness issues on his own time. She flipped to the questions page of her own printouts. "Tell me who you know that you think would be helpful in this project?"

Not that it entirely stopped his fidgeting, but eventually Austin did shrug back one shoulder, then the next, and then both at once, in case she'd missed it, and slid open his cell phone. "My pal Ty works in the School of Communication.

He lived across the hall from me the year I was in the dorms, and he worked with me a lot on the Pier Three Studios. I was thinking it's the kind of thing that would be perfect for a senior project, or an internship, something like that. I think he'd be up for working along those lines with his students. Also, there's Sofia, who runs one of the art studios on campus. I don't remember the way she's got her title or anything, but she and Callie are really good friends. You know Callie?"

She did not roll her eyes, because she supposed it could be possible, despite her friendships with Sally and with Austin's cousin Noah, that she stayed ignorant of all the genius artists who came to town and upended Austin's brother's world. "I know Callie, yeah."

He flushed again, turning his skin from generic beach bro white to lacy pink. It seemed even his year-round tan wasn't enough to dampen on all that color. "Yeah. Okay, so she's happy to connect me with Sofia and get some sort of tie-in from her. Maybe she and Ty would work together and turn it into some sort of project for credit."

So his ideas were not bad. Gold star to him.

She jotted down the particulars and asked a few clarifying questions and paid no heed to the way he grimaced and proclaimed there was no point in following through on his ideas since, probably she had all of the contacts and approaches worked out already.

Instead, she slid his copies of the plan back to her side of the table and filled in their respective names, adding his new ideas where they seem the most logical. He craned his neck enough to see what she was doing, then sat back and let his grin reemerge. "So you like it?"

"Do you need a cookie? I didn't notice you going out of your way to tell me if you liked my ideas."

There went his hand through his hair again, releasing another dust cloud. He clenched his fist and shoved it back under his thigh. "Crap, that was rude of me. I shouldn't just suppose you know that I recognize how genius you are. Sorry. Yeah, you, uh, your brilliance is on display, Leyla. Thank you for all the work you put in here. Sorry I went off on you like that before. That was a real pile of defensive crap to throw at you, and you already gave up so much of your free time to volunteer for this, and put together these solid ideas."

Well, hell. One thing Leyla appreciated was a genuine moment of learning when she didn't have to be the teacher. She smiled and slid his copy back at him. "We're cool. Look this over. Any changes? Anything we need to switch up, add on, or take away?"

Austin slouched a little while he read, that too-bright grin gone, as well as his bashful face. Not that she cared one way or the other if she got a glimpse of some kind of true side of him. It was a little interesting, in an anthropological kind of way. But anthropology wasn't her science. And getting bogged down in the details of Austin Wells's expressions wasn't gonna save the oceans. So, she focused on compiling their notes and establishing an agenda and date for their next meeting. "I was thinking Friday afternoon, if you're free?"

He tapped around his papers a bit. "Yeah. Two-ish?"

She winced when she checked her own calendar. "Fucking Chad," she muttered. Which she could admit was not much of an answer.

"Is Chad a person?"

She snorted. "He likes to think so."

Austin didn't know who this Chad was, but he hated him. It was cliche, sure, the way his protective nature whirled into action when Leyla grimaced about the guy. He reminded his innate responses that Leyla knew more about protecting her own self than he could ever hope to glean. She especially didn't need his growly act reminding her that he was probably as tedious as ... as whatever it was about this guy that set her on high alert.

He reminded himself to chill the hell out and play at being neutral when he said, "And is Chad a problem for scheduling our next project meeting?"

"He's a problem for so many more reasons than that. But yes, that, too."

"What's his deal?"

"Lord knows. We interned at the Dunlavy Institute together last summer, and his life goal is to prove he's better than me so they offer him the only full-time position they're hiring for."

"Yeah, but he can't actually be better than you. Don't the people in this Dunlavy Institute have any clue?"

The tip-tilt of her eyes hinted at a smile that didn't quite bloom on her mouth. It was like watching a cranking set building from the takeoff zone, knowing he would soon pop up and skim the lip of the wave. If only he had the skills to drop down into Leyla's tides.

"They'll learn. I just got to execute a couple things off my fight the patriarchy task list in the process. But that means Friday is out. Can you swing Saturday before noon?"

He was the one to grimace when he finished checking all his calendars.

She shrugged. "I expect weekends are busy for the cafe. You're working, probably?"

"No, I ..." He hesitated, but she wasn't likely to blab to his family. "I have a class."

He didn't know what she was expecting when she glanced around his apartment. Probably her place was full of over-flowing bookshelves and strewn desks and one of those thick university-branded mugs stuffed with writing implements. All she would see in his apartment was his big sofa facing his big TV and gaming system. A bunch of electronics, and not so much as a magazine laying around. "I keep my backpack in my bedroom."

The look she gave him when he blurted that out was clue number one that she wasn't thinking all those derogatory things he was imagining. Clue two was Leyla asking, "Is the backpack something we need for the Expo project?"

He caught himself chewing the inside of his cheek and forced a smile. "No, nothing like that. I was guessing that your apartment might not be so ..."

"Uncluttered?"

"No, but: devoid of any sign of brainy pursuits?"

"Brainy pursuits?"

"Like, not just video games and yoga mats. You probably have, I don't know, notebooks and a dictionary and a white board and an external hard drive to backup all your research."

She pressed her lips together and he promised his brain he could spend time—later—contemplating what it would feel like to be on the receiving end of all that luscious mobile pressure.

"Yeah, so my books and all that, I just keep in my room." He shifted a little to gesture towards his bedroom. Fuck. *Bedroom, his bed. Leyla, in his bed.* He went back to looking at the way she'd written his name beside the jobs she thought he was capable of doing.

"Are you prescient or something?"

He quick lifted his gaze to hers.

"I'm amazed. You just went and described my place perfectly. Except you did leave out the side table where I have a chessboard set up on a lazy susan so I can spin it back and forth as I play against myself. That's an important part of my quest to constantly sharpen my mind."

Oh hell, she was sniping at him. He'd said something rude

or foolish again. Lips, bed, now something about her place. Her books.

"Sorry. I don't mean to be down on your home decor."

"Or what you imagined my home decor to be."

"Right, that. I ..." He cleared his throat. "We get students in here a lot, being this close to campus? And you know I'm the super, so when I'm in their apartments for something, I notice how they're averaged out to be different from how my place is. But I'm not trying to say that—"

"I'm boring?" She flicked her eyes at his, and he was probably blushing again with the effort of not countering her claim with detailed descriptions of all the things he'd imagined her life to be like. Lately he'd convinced himself her bedding would be yellow, but that was because he couldn't stop thinking about the way a shirt she'd worn to Pier Three a few weeks back set off the glowing skin of her neck and collarbones. When he'd been at the hardware store picking up more mud and tape for his bathroom remodel, he'd let himself gather paint samples of the cool blues and sage greens he dreamed would complement her sheets.

So, yeah, he was better off keeping his mouth shut. "Sorry," he muttered.

"I get it. Why would you think different? As far as you know, all I ever do is teach and work on my master's."

He damned his need to contradict her, and the odds of doing so without revealing what a vault his otherwise flighty memory was about everything to do with her. "Sure, the degree obviously keeps you busy, but you surf. And you come to bonfires some. Hang out with Noah and Sally. And I know I've seen you in Pier Three with other friends, just being together. Not in a study group or whatever."

Fuck.

When she raised her eyebrows, they arched up in such elegant swoops, hovering above the top rims of her glasses.

He needed to not be staring. He turned back to his calendars. "So, sorry, yeah, I've got class from nine to eleven on Saturday morning."

"Okay." Her voice had a very 'leave that conversation in the past and move on' tone. "We can work around that. Maybe first thing? We can meet at Grinds so you're on campus already? Or I'll be in the library that afternoon, you could find me there after your class."

"No, I'm ... over in San Jose. At the community college." He cleared his throat, then sighed. "It's not a big thing, but could you not mention it to my family? I haven't told them yet, but I'm working on my associate's degree."

Chapter Seven

He looked all embarrassed again, and the thing about not mentioning his classes to his family put a certain amount of alert in her mind. Her own family was weighed down sometimes with intellectual snobbery. In particular, her mom's side was top to toe full of people with advanced degrees, while her dad's side—not so much. Mom's mama, along with a couple of her cousins on that side, were less than sweet about how they judged Dad's sister and brother for not striving enough. "I won't share your private business, don't worry."

Maybe her turn-about to sympathy was a little much after their earlier interactions, because he rapid-fired words again. "I'm not embarrassed. I'll tell them eventually. I don't feel like getting into it with them just yet, but it'll happen. When I'm ready."

She held up a palm to halt him. "I'm not into putting on a rash guard just to interact with you, Austin, so can you be calm? I can respect your business without you jumping to the conclusion I have opinions on it."

He nodded, and flashed his crooked canine half-smile that surely kept his tip jar full.

"Anyway, it's no problem to plan our work around your classes. And if you ever do want to access the University Library, let me know. I can get a pass from Sally without telling her who it's for."

She could practically hear his lungs compress as he shrank into stillness. "I don't mind Sally knowing. Like I said, I'll tell my family later. But if they knew I was taking classes, they'd knot themselves up trying to take things like this project off my plate."

"And that's a bad thing?" She knew plenty of peers without supportive families. The way he sounded, those people were the better off ones.

He pulled one of his scribbled up sticky notes and started to fold it, using his thumbnail to plant creases as he worked.

"They'll all be overjoyed, don't get me wrong." His voice took on a deeper, almost gruff tone. "Better late than never. And an associate's degree, that's ... not bad. Not at all."

He kept working the sticky note until he'd transformed it into a butterfly. The sharp lines and assured moves were hints the origami was something he turned to often. His cynical huff sent the creature fluttering to the edge of the table, but his voice took back its usual cadence. "They'll be over the moon, but also, so sure that it's gonna be too much for me. Next thing I know, Abraham will leave his trip with Callie early to take over my shifts, and my dad'll change the password on the building maintenance portal so I can't access it, and who knows what Alicia will tell Mateo about my inability to focus on my degree and Surfside Swell both. Or, no—she'll go and plot with the family that I should be freed of my paid work, but keep up this gig with you. Because you'll be a good influence on me, with all your fascinating brilliance, and I can learn a bunch by watching the way you navigate the world."

Leyla snagged the paper butterfly and studied it. Even with Austin's folded scribbles making them not proper mirror image wings, it was cute. A little offbeat, a little charming. Interesting and worth looking at.

Suffice to say, she'd never transformed her notes into something artsy once in her life.

"If your sister claimed I've got fascinating brilliance, she was overstating things. I'm like a hundred other grad students. All I do is navigate my teaching load and capstone schedule. You said yourself, you've seen all those carbon copy student apartments. Books, more books, and papers, and more papers."

Hell, she hadn't even color-coded the lists she'd brought to their meeting. Forget not being artsy, she wasn't showing any signs of the kinds of creativity that could give her an edge against the Chads of the world. And since when had she stopped making that kind of effort? Plain black text might work for her male peers, but she knew enough about ingrained bias to know people would be more receptive to her work if it had a pretty gloss on it.

The butterfly's messy ink was green. And Austin's notes on her monochrome sheaf of detailed, not-at-all-offbeat project management? All written in either purple or red. She'd not even seen him bringing multiple pen colors to the table. For all that his apartment was basic single straight man blah, he'd made full and festive use of his office supplies.

"What are you getting your degree in?"

"Alicia's not the one who says you're fascinating and brilliant. That's me."

Oh fuck oh fuck oh fuck.

He cleared his throat and tried again. "Communications. It's an AA in Communications. Once I built the studios— above the cafe, you know? Of course you know, Alicia took you up there the other day. So. I was talking a bunch with my friend Ty, that's the audio engineer I mentioned earlier. And I took some management classes when I—before I dropped out. Twelve credits shy of my BA, that's what my family will say when they know I'm doing this. Twelve credits, Dad always repeats, but that never accounts for how I changed majors twice once I was finally forced to declare. I could've spent that last semester on campus day in and day out, but it wouldn't have gotten me a degree, which Dad conveniently forgets. And so I was talking to Ty and it made me realize I care enough about the music and podcast stuff that I could probably stick with a program long enough for it to be useful, especially since I remember a lot of that management coursework. Plus, the way I'm wired, if it's useful, I don't care as much how hard something is? I mean, I'm no good at school, that's always been true for me. But the hard parts don't bug me as much when I'm interested in something, maybe?"

She nodded, which seemed unlikely given that he wasn't making any sense. But then she asked, "Do you think there's part of you that is more determined to get through it exactly because it's difficult for you? That you're proving something to yourself?"

He gulped down the shock of being seen so pointedly. And by Leyla, of all the humans on the planet. "I, um, maybe so? When Ty first mentioned the course I dismissed it, but then I looked at all the requirements and how much time it would take, and ... Yeah. Probably, yeah. I probably want to do it even more because it's hard."

And if that wasn't the most full-gut cringe stream of nonsense, he'd night surf without his board leashed to his ankle. First, he blurts out how he's the one fascinated by her, then he rambles about how he likes it to be hard.

Points to him for not saying, "You have the sexiest shoulders in existence and I need your lips on mine," but Leyla was way too smart not to get his subtext.

She reached for his wrist, drawing it towards her and rotating so his hand rested palm up in the middle of the table. For the first time in maybe the entire day, he went still, watching while she lifted the butterfly with her other hand.

The fact she was still holding the suddenly sensitive skin of his inner wrist was a vital moment he was never going to forget.

She set the paper creation in the bowl of his hand, her lovely fingers dragging just a little across his thumb as she brought them back to where she could lean towards him, chin on fist. He was maybe not breathing, but that was okay. Breathing was overrated.

"So the degree. Yeah. I guess I picked it partly because it's hard, and also maybe when I get through all the coursework, I'll have figured out how to come up with more good ideas that are worth exploring, instead of losing them in my 'bit of this, bit of that energy,' as my brother called it once. I think I can maybe get to a point where I can figure out how to explain why some of my ideas are worth doing."

She couldn't mean it, the way she held his whole self captive with two fingers on his wrist. She just wanted to grab his attention for whatever she was going to say next.

That was familiar enough, from his whole life of people trying to force him to focus. It was only the electric current of her fingertips on his pulse that was different. And he could ignore that. Well, he couldn't ignore it; it was part of his soul now. But he could remind himself to set it aside and pay attention to her words.

"I'm not saying I know you well enough to pass judgment on every proposal you've ever made, but we've been talking for the past twenty minutes and you've said a half-dozen good ideas I'd never thought of. Plus, I do know that Pier Three

Studios wasn't only something you constructed—it was your idea to start with. And you had to talk to your sister and brother into it, right?"

He swallowed down a mingled lump of embarrassment, shame, and exultation. "I mean, it's because I knew Ty. One of them would have thought of it, if they knew him and heard him talking about how the university was restricting access to their studios for anyone but undergrads."

"Would they have? If that's true, they must have jumped on board as soon as you explained it, right?" Those eyebrow of hers quirked over the edge of her glasses again, and he was not the man to hide or lie at her challenge.

Normally, yeah. Running and hiding: his way through the world. But Leyla challenged that side of him.

Damn, if she would just challenge him twenty-four seven, what a man he would become. Except, none of that was her job. If he wanted to be a different kind of man, that was on him. And hell, if showing himself to her as that new guy wasn't a fascinating idea he'd be mulling over later in lieu of sleep.

"I had to put together a presentation and back it up with data and research to prove to them my instincts were right."

She full-on smiled at him, and if his heart was that sticky butterfly in his hand, it would have taken wing and circled until it found a resting place somewhere on her. Shoulders, maybe. Or in one of the coils of her hair. He could weave his little butterfly legs in so it'd be impossible to lose her, even while she was flowing in the ocean or snuggled up in those imaginary sunrise yellow sheets of hers.

But the butterfly was inert, and it wasn't her duty to make it fly, even in his imagination.

"Thanks." It wasn't nearly enough to express his full body rift from the things he'd always believed, about his being too scattered to be useful. Even if he did still need to work on his follow through.

"Seriously, Leyla. Thanks again. It's been too long since I questioned the stories I tell about myself." He lifted the butterfly and tucked the wing under the band of her sports watch, then he drew his hand from hers.

Not her job to tell him he wasn't entirely full of shit. That was an orange sharpie on pink sticky kind of thought, so he snagged the right supplies and scribbled it on a note he then tacked to the back of the festival paperwork.

"So, Saturday early, or when?"

She tapped to wake her phone and they worked out a time and Austin escorted her to the door before he found himself begging her to reframe every single thing he or his family had ever said about him.

Chapter Eight

"Leyla!" Somehow Dean Tyler cried her name with more surprised than delight.

She'd made an appointment with him directly, and showed up two minutes before her email had promised, so she wasn't loving how he projected an air of amazement to find her sitting across from his office desk. Not that she didn't appreciate the shift from his usual proprietorial air.

"Dr. Thibideaux was just telling me about your tide pool project. I'm so pleased. I'd warned him to expect great things from you, after all."

And there it was.

Yes, the man had been her undergrad thesis advisor, and had almost more industry connections than the rest of the faculty combined. And yes, he'd written her recommendation to grad school, winking all the while like her concerns about getting in were cute rather than based on her through research about requirements and available spaces.

But he always had to act like her successes were a feather in his cap, instead of her own. The Dean's attitude towards her could have been worse. Patronizing, or paternalistic. But it didn't make her any happier to place her aggravations with him on a sliding scale.

In just a few more months, she'd have her degree, and hopefully her job, and then none of her life would involve dealing directly with the administration. Meanwhile, she played the game. They chatted about her thesis, and the impact the project was making already, and she let slide at least five more comments that somebody unfamiliar with the subtext might not have heard as pointed.

Leyla, though, knew all of the subtext. She knew the subtext to the subtext.

Strategizing with Sally, they'd decided on her bringing up the committee before mentioning the Expo. Get the Dean so caught up in the idea he could present her like his prize Black grad student to the committee, that he'd incidentally agree to help with the Expo without giving himself too much over-thinking time. And it seemed to pan out. She mentioned hearing about the committee and that she thought it was an initiative with plenty of potential.

As soon as he showed signs of wanting to dive deep into the details, Leyla pulled out her Expo presentation. "I'm so curious to learn more, but with my capstone and this other project, I've got to be careful not to overextend myself. So, I can focus on my capstone as much as I need to, especially after the things we discussed."

Leyla hadn't spent as much of her life as possible near oceans without figuring out a thing or two about baiting hooks.

She gave the Expo presentation a considering look before pausing, then broke into a bright smile and handed it over. "I don't think this has to take up so much of my time, though. Not if I can get it sewn up fairly quickly. That's what I want to ask your advice about." She layered on a few more kudos about his savvy within the administration, and acted in general like she wasn't across the desk from him hoping he'd take over immediately. She just needed his insider knowledge of what to do next, etc.

After a bit more nonsense about his know-how, an oblique reference to the dean of the College of Nursing, who everybody knew was Tyler's faculty nemesis, and a mention that if he flipped to page three he'd see how the university had, in the past, used similar connections to the town to build their profile. She even threw in a couple of DEIA buzz words in case he forgot about the committee help he wanted.

She knew she didn't have to be as subtle as all that. Dean Tyler was no fool. But part of getting his buy-in was proving that she and he both knew exactly where all the quid pro quo lines lay.

After he introduced Ty to Sofia—well, made their knowledge of each other a bit tighter, since they sort of knew each other in passing—and they all talked through ideas for using the Expo to fuel some creative student projects, everything devolved to chit chat while they waited for Leyla to come join them.

Sofia went to order herself some lunch. Ty reached over and flattened his palm on Austin's forearm. "You're vibrating."

"Oh, sorry."

"I wouldn't mind but the syncopation is way off. So, something's going on with you?"

He tipped his sunglasses down over his eyes and shrugged. "Nope. I'm the same as always, you know me. No bad news, no good news, just working to get this project in full swing."

"How's your classes?"

He chanced a glance at Sofia, who was chatting with the

line chef about bell peppers or white sauce or something. "It's all good, but, thing is, I haven't told my family yet. So, I don't want to put Sofia in an awkward position."

If they'd had more time before Sofia carried her plate back towards them, he'd have probably just explained all of his issues about keeping it private. Ty knew some of it already, from the days they'd been at university together. Hell, he'd been the one to mention the associate's degree over at San Jose. Still, it surprised him to realize he'd be amenable to the conversation.

Seemed like having opened up a little bit about it with Leyla pointed his mind in the direction of sharing with everybody. Well, not everybody—sure as fuck not with Alicia or Abraham. But he took that morsel of surprising new self-knowledge away to mess with another time.

He looked up to say something to Sofia and found himself absorbing how all the light in the room had concentrated on Leyla when she walked in. She was wearing business lady pants and a geometric print shirt topped with a kind of structured cardigan or really loose blazer that was the same purpley-pink as her lipstick. Or probably she matched her lipstick to her coat, not the other way around, but either way, it wasn't till Ty jiggled his wrist a little that Austin realized he'd gone still.

"And there's nothing up with you," Ty uttered, but quietly enough, he hoped, that only Austin heard.

He made all the introductions and Ty proved he was a good friend by jumping in to give Leyla the rundown on what they'd been scheming. After that, she and the others kind of ran with the conversation, which gave him a couple of minutes to form some saliva back into his mouth. When he finally spoke up and offered to get her a latte or some such, she laughed, which set him spinning down out of control again.

"I don't think Campus Grinds is equipped to provide me with a latte, thanks anyway. Did you think it was a coincidence, so many people from campus showing up at Pier Three? We don't go just to give you more people to flirt with."

He was too parched to do much more than some kind of half-shrug, half-nod bullshit that made no sense to him. He didn't expect it would make much sense to her either. But: who else did Leyla suspect he was flirting with? According to his brother, his sister—everyone, even his employees and at least three of his regulars—Leyla was the only one he ever flirted with. And his tendency in that regard was way beyond obvious.

She couldn't really think he'd spent as much time thinking about anyone else as he did about her, could she? Because, yeah, she wouldn't have any intel regarding what he acted like when she wasn't around, but maybe she still didn't know that she was something special to him?

His crush was all too one-sided. He knew that. Once he actually braved asking Abraham if his attention to her bordered on creepy or rude. Not that Abe helped. He just laughed, then when Austin didn't join in, told him if he was that concerned about it, he should maybe check in with Alicia.

Of course, that just sobered them both the fuck up, because it reminded them what their sister had been through at her job before they started Pier Three. Neither of them liked to ruminate on that shit. Then Abe offered to ask Callie about it, and Austin had to shut the conversation down fast as anything. He didn't want his brother turning him into a conversational focus with his girlfriend.

And if they were gonna do it anyway, he didn't want to know shit about what they'd conclude together.

The unfortunate thing was, that left him without a whole lot of options when it came to knowing if he should lock his feelings for Leyla in a vault, or what. He'd kind of hoped that everyone teasing him about how he turned upside down and bounced into the stratosphere when she was around, meant that she'd had the opportunity to pick up what he was laying down.

If she wanted.

Maybe that was too chickenshit of him, though. Maybe not being direct meant he was putting all the burden on her to interpret his nonsense. And that sure as shit did not sound like a sexy kind of thing to do to the woman who he was not so subtly pining over.

Under the table, Ty kicked at his ankle. He blinked to bring his thoughts back on the conversation around them, and sorted through any vestiges that he'd noticed to realize they'd all agreed on a provisional plan, and had a few new ideas to add to the mix.

He threw a grateful smile Ty's way and blurted out some bullshit that didn't linger in his head before it hit his tongue. "What about making a podcast about the process of putting on our first Expo? I could do interviews with everyone who's helping out. We can run surveys about, I don't know, whatever. Slogans the students come up with, or graphics, to see how the community responds to them. If that's not too harsh on the students. People are more engaged if you give them something to vote on. I think I can put it together in the free time at Pier Three Studios. We'd not be looking for a huge reach, but maybe the university would link to it. Probably I can do it for my Interpersonal Communication class project. Unless you all think it's not worth it? No one needs my voice in a podcast, right? So. But your stuff is great. I like what you said about the graphics, so, yeah that sounds amazing."

Now Leyla was the one nudging him under the table. "Hey, you're doing it again."

"Sorry?"

"Coming up with an idea and then talking yourself out of it before you can let anybody else speak. Don't be so sure it's not worth exploring."

Oh hell. He'd absolutely done that again, just like she'd said. His face was probably purple with embarrassment. He crossed his arms to stop himself from burying his face in his hands. No wonder she wasn't interested in any of the thousand times he'd flirted at her.

"Yeah, sorry."

Ty was looking between them. "Hey, I gotta head out, man. Sofia, you want me to walk you back toward the art center?"

Chapter Nine

Austin's friends took off, not without some significant-seeming looks exchanged between him and Ty.

He was holding himself oddly still, and some sneaky sneak in her brain suggested it was because he regretted introducing her to his friends, and maybe felt like all this was turning into some untoward burden that he'd had enough of before they'd hardly begun. That he was talking himself out of his podcast idea, not because of any sort of insecurity, but because he realized halfway through pitching it that the idea might force him to spend a little more time dealing with her and her tedious timelines and objectives and goal setting strategies.

"You sure I can't get you a drink? Maybe iced tea, or some ..." He swiveled halfway around to take in the menu board. "Salad?"

"I tend to not drink salads."

His gaze caught on her as he twisted back, and she bit back on explaining that it was a joke, because hell if she was gonna prove herself to be another whole level of boring by explaining what passed as her jokes.

He blinked twice and slouched with one arm over the back

of the chair, grinning. "That feels like a challenge. I can make it a smoothie, with kale of course. Maybe some spinach. Oh, cucumber! Cashew milk and ... beets? Yeah, beets. Blueberries and beets, and voila: drinkable salad."

His keen brown eyes went all dancing and shit, and all the sudden they were laughing together. It went some way to making that brain sneak go slinking underground.

"So, no salad?"

"I can't say that I've ever been all that tempted by the offerings in this place."

"After all the times you've surfed up to my takeout window, I kind of suspected. But I apologize about making you meet us here. It was kind of central for the others."

"It's not like I've never eaten here. But if you're up for a little walk, we could head back to mine. I can offer you some hot tea?"

He was scooping up the assorted papers and writing implements into his backpack before she was done asking. "You live on campus?"

She led the way out. "Yeah, grad student housing. It's a three bedroom, which is whatever. But my roommates are good folk. They sometimes wish I wasn't quite so early a riser, but otherwise we get on pretty well."

"The curse of living with a surfer. Abraham used to gripe mightily about it, until I talked our parents into letting me store my quiver in their garage. A lot less dinging my boards in the hallway that way. But Mom and Dad have the only garage unit in the whole complex, and I have it half-commandeered for workshop purposes, so they always claimed there was no room. Except they both switched to these little electric cars, and while I was rearranging the space to install their charging stations, I snuck in a rack that just so happens to be the right size to hold my boards. Mom was more ticked than Dad, but Abraham made it clear he was pretty happy about the whole situation, so that took care of her."

She made some kind of amused noise that lit up the three or four iotas of his body not already buzzing from being in her proximity. "Your brother's a bit of a mama's boy?"

"Yeah, not in a bad way. Just, they've got a bond. She took on a lot of the logistics, and I guess the emotional and mental load of ..." Austin lifted his left arm and waggled it, which Leyla took to be a reference to his brother's prosthetic limb. "Dad explained to me once that even though any of her parental fears about her baby being bullied, or how he'd navigate situations at school, any of that, were pretty much worked out by the time he was seven or eight, it didn't stop any the worries from hanging out in her heart. So even though she didn't have to storm the elementary school gates to protect anyone, there's still this soft spot in her that glows extra bright when it's clear Abraham's feeling happy."

It was a sweet enough story, and Leyla could relate to the way her own parents got extra shiny about any kind of triumph of hers or her sister's, but it seemed like there was a bit to unpack there about Austin, and maybe about Alicia, and about their relationship with their mom. None of her affair.

She led him up to her second-floor apartment. He was looking around the place like he was confused. She couldn't tell if she should be amused or offended by the look on his face. "Something to say?"

"No yellow."

"Is that a safe word?"

"A safe ... Wha?"

He went purple, and she might have, too, if she hadn't had the grace of melanin to hide her embarrassment.

"No, it's not that, I wouldn't. I—" He seemed to literally

bite his own tongue, if the way his jaw stilled and he winced was any indication.

She raised her eyebrows at him, waiting for an explanation.

"When I imagined your place, I imagined you'd decorate it with yellow. Or maybe that daybreak orange that happens in the sky, like ten minutes after the sun rises over the foothills, you know the one?"

Not so she'd have ever described it that way herself, but as soon as he mentioned it, she could picture it exactly. But now she was flustered over this whole concept. "You thought about what my home would look like, not just jokes about my chess board?"

"It's just, you've got that one yellow-orange shirt? And it makes your skin glow extra pretty?"

He said it like a question, and her face must have questioned him right back before she could think to blank it.

Austin dropped his backpack beside the sofa and stepped towards her. "I was thinking back there, maybe you don't know how much I like you." He reeled back after blurting that and froze a sec, watching her. "I know you don't need me on this project, and I know you probably don't want to deal with my messy emotions when you're just trying to finish your degree. And no matter how much everyone says I'm obvious —maybe I am obvious, maybe you've know this already, and not responding to it is your actual response. Which, I get that. It's a hundred percent, a thousand percent valid. Obviously. That's probably the situation, too. That you know about my massive crush, and just ignore it out of politeness. Which I understand. Completely. There's no reason you wouldn't be hoping I would get the hint and back down, but I had this sudden idea. You know how I am with my sudden ideas. It was that if you didn't know, I was just causing myself a silly amount of pain by hoping you'd figure it out and respond. But that's not proactive, right? That's me being passive and lazy and throwing the burden on you. So, my idea that came to me was that I should just say it. I should just tell you how much I adore you, and then it it's out in the open. So, I now know that you know, and whatever you choose to do or not do ... I mean, obviously, not doing is completely your right and I will go if I'm making you uncomfortable."

She shut him up with a kiss.

Leyla was kissing him. *Leyla*.

Leyla Robinson.

Leyla Robinson relaxing her strong warrior's body against him.

Against him. Against Austin Wells. Leyla Robinson kissing Austin Wells.

She drew back for a sec and took him in, made a question noise as she licked her lips. He gave a fraction of a nod, and she brought her lips back to his, and it was everything, her kissing him.

He drew his hand over her hair, her shoulder (her *shoulder!*), down her arm to interlink their fingers, because he needed to touch her. He needed to anchor himself in her brilliance and her beauty, but he couldn't get carried away. She was probably going to stop him soon, so he wouldn't let his hands get carried away like they wanted. Like he wanted. Like he wanted her to do to him.

And even while he thought it, she scraped her other hand over his scalp and tightened it at the back of his head, keeping them together. As if he had any intention of being anywhere but exactly in this spot. He wrapped his arm around her waist. God, the muscles, the curves, the electricity.

He was dead from joy, but not wholly dead. He wouldn't allow that to happen. Not when Leyla Robinson's beautiful lush lips moved on his, and his whole universe was her warmth and her softness and her strength and her scent and the mind-boggling, earth-shaking fact that Leyla Robinson had chosen to kiss him.

She was pure magic to him and he was bewitched. The whole situation unreal. Questions later. Not now. Later.

Now, he was entirely at Leyla's disposal. And entirely tumbled over how telling her what he felt had led, not to complete rejection, but to her hand in his, and to all this unreal, perfect, life-affirming kissing.

His hand skimmed the curve of her hip and just the thought of her strong surfer's thighs and ass had him growling and pressing closer. It was some kind of trick, he knew it had to be, because since when did he live a life that had room in it for his dick to harden against Leyla's stomach, while her blunt nails scraped his spine?

That wasn't anything but a dream, and he was going to live in it for as long as possible, because he just goddamn wanted it so much.

Her mouth opened further under his, and he was so ready. He was so, so ready to press into her. To let his tongue continue to explore the delicacy and beauty of her mouth. And maybe she was, too? He'd hardly dared imagine being in a situation that was so beyond, so blissful.

Which is why he shouldn't have been surprised when Leyla dropped her hand to his shoulder and pulled back. "No, sorry."

No, sorry.

No.

Of course that's what Leyla would say within seconds of kissing him.

"All right." He retreated to her doorway, which along with everything else, gave him a view of the backpack he'd left sitting by her sofa. But it was next to her, and she had pushed him away, so it didn't matter. He didn't need his backpack.

"Austin?" She didn't sound any surer than he was about meeting his eyes, but he wasn't going to deny her her say. Even though it meant standing there with his damned flagging erection on display, in the awareness that she'd looked at the bulge before swallowing and getting on with her rejection.

Maybe, later, it would be a balm to his soul that she didn't let whatever annoyance or disgust she felt charge her words. Except later, he knew, he would also be reminding himself that she'd welcomed him into her home, and he'd responded by throwing himself at her, and now she was a woman alone, wanting to ease the strong young man out of her space without escalating anything.

She took a really, really careful breath, and he couldn't move, because if he moved—if he spoke—she might see it as a sign that he wouldn't go peaceably. He stuck his hands in his pockets and nodded, waiting for her to speak. Not that he could have braced himself entirely for what she ended up saying.

"It's not you. You're nice, I'm not trying to deny that. But you were just ... God, Austin, you were talking so much. The way you always do. I shouldn't have handled it that way, but I needed you to be quiet."

She winced, and that was it. That was all he could process. Those lips he'd been kissing. That face he wanted to cradle and treasure and memorize. Those eyes working hard to not blink as she gauged whether he would react badly.

He swallowed. "I overstepped. That's on me. You don't need to say anything more." He nodded his farewells, fumbled for the door behind him, and left before, he hoped, she could see that he was about to cry.

Chapter Ten

She didn't know what to do, so she phoned her sister.

"Hey, Sis. Let me guess: Chad driving you up a wall again?"

"No. Well, yes, obviously that's how he rolls. But, no. I'm ..." She blew out a breath. "Okay. You got a minute?"

Zora snorted. "Points to you."

"Oh, shush." They'd called each other at all hours for years now, but it was only once Zora booed up and moved in with her partner that suddenly Leyla was ever so kindly reminded that sometimes her calls were an interruption.

If it was just the times her sister was getting some, it'd be no big deal. Neither had qualms about sending the other to voicemail, whether it was for work or class or date time. But Zora and Lance living together meant, apparently, any time could be interrupting time. Maybe they were cooking together, or streaming a show, or debating some nonsense on social media. Used to be, Leyla could call Zora during any of those circumstances, and her sister would stop what she was doing or else fold her into whatever was happening. But now she had always check she wasn't somehow imposing on Zora and Lance's time together.

It got so she found herself waiting for Zora to initiate their near-daily calls, until she realized how she was turning her power over unprovoked, and made herself find a way to restore their connection without causing any undue stress on the relationship. It helped that she had no problem with Lance. The guy passed all the tests she could imagined for her sister. But she wouldn't say she loved how his constant presence in life impacted their sister vibe.

"What did that useless white boy do?"

"He's not useless."

"Excuse me. We're talking about the same Chad who's so at a loss for good sense that he can only figure out how to pass a class by taking credit for your work? The one who didn't back down even when you had timestamps showing you're the one who developed the prototype he based his solution on?"

Her whole self was a rolling-eyes gif. At least she'd had peer support her when she went to the prof, which had made navigating the whole situation easier. "Oh, that useless white guy. No, nothing's changed there. Well, nothing official. I've gone and volunteered myself for a committee that'll put me front and center on the Dean's radar, and when he finds out he'll probably do his usual and claim I'm playing the minority card. I figure as long as I'm prepared, I can handle myself against that nonsense."

"Baby, you can handle yourself no matter how unprepared you are. You're just that good."

Leyla hadn't realized she'd needed the affirmation. She sank onto the sofa, tugging Austin's backpack up into her lap. Which was probably something she should question about herself. Especially once she caught herself sniffing the damn thing. No backpack in the world was worth tenderly cradling and sniffing like she might catch a hint of Austin's coconut coffee scent.

"Fuck," she said, dropping her head back and closing her eyes.

"What's happening? You have a problem with some other white boy? Tell big sis everything."

"He's not ... well, yes, he's white, but that's not the point."

"Oh, what's the point?"

"I have shit to do, Zora."

"And your to-do list doesn't include this new entanglement with some random man off the street?"

"He's not off the street. He's a cousin of my friend Noah, from the surf shop."

Zora snickered. "You and your surfing. You would have friends from the surf shop."

"Excuse me." She put on her lecture hall voice. "Surfing is a growing sport among the Black community and I am proud to be subverting people's expectations when they see me in the waves."

"Okay, okay, your kudos are duly noted. What's the thing that's got you in a tizzy then, if not the machinations of the inestimable Chad?"

"Inestimable Chad. Ha. I can still tell you're teasing me, even when you use ten dollar words, Zora Robinson."

"I can still tell that you're avoiding the exact topic you called me to discuss, even when you pick on my diction, Leyla Robinson."

She tsked through her teeth, which made Zora laugh, which made Lance mumble something in the background. She ate the tiniest snippet of jealousy about her sister's relationship. Not over Lance himself, but the pure fact of Zora having him poked some measly part of her.

She wasn't giving that bitterness any heed. Instead, she laid out all the facts in a methodical way. Volunteering to help with the Expo, making strategies and having meetings, and, well, there was nothing methodical about the next part. So, even though it made her curse herself, she found herself blathering.

"He does this thing where he comes up with an idea. It's like he has a thought and then starts to explain it and during the explanation, manages to talk himself out of it, all convinced suddenly it's a bad idea."

"Yeah? And what bad idea did he share that made you call me all flustered?"

She was hugging his goddamn backpack again. Who does that? Thing was hardly a teddy bear. "He told me he's had this huge crush on me, which, are we grown or not? A crush? And then he started to explain why, in great detail, I would have no use for his feelings. Going on about me being too good for him and how I have more important things to do."

"Smart man. You are too good for him. You're too good for everyone. And so? What'd he do? He's not still standing right there watching you confess all this, is he? Cause that's a little unkind, Sis."

"No, of course not. I couldn't let him keep going on about how amazing I am. It was embarrassing." Her voice dropped to a mutter. "So I kissed him."

Zora's laugh was so loud Leyla worried she would set off the oversensitive alarm of the car parked below her window. "Oh you did, did you? And did that shush our fine young friend? What's his name, by the way? I can't keep thinking of him as the anti-Chad when you've had your tongue down his throat. Just saying."

She sighed. "Austin. His name's Austin."

"Right. Classic. And when was this?"

She had to lift her glasses to pinch the bridge of her nose. "Like ten minutes ago."

"And he's not still in your apartment? He's not standing right there feeling you up while we talk?"

"You're not funny, Zora."

"I'm pretty funny."

"Not when you're talking about me, you're not. Save your wit for Lance."

"No fear. My man knows I'm the funniest."

Lance called out his background agreement.

"Bye, Zora."

She didn't actually hang up on her. It wouldn't have done any good, since her sister would have proceeded to blow up her phone until she relented and allowed the interrogation.

She only tried to protest until Zora rightly said, "If you weren't ready to tell me exactly how you feel, you wouldn't have phoned. Stop fronting and confess. You like this guy?"

Leyla really needed to stop cradling Austin's backpack. "You know I don't have dating on my radar."

"Do not start telling me you don't have time for this," Zora chided. "You just finished telling me last week how far ahead you are on your capstone deadline. And if I remember details correctly, which let's admit that I surely do, you already spend half your free time in this Austin's vicinity, between his coffee shop and you all surfing and the bonfires you like to hang out at with your surf shop friend Noah."

"It's not like you've never surfed."

"And I appreciate you forcing me to all those lessons, but that is not my particular passion. Some of us desert girls are very happy with where we were planted."

Until that afternoon, Leyla would have said she was very happy with where she'd transplanted herself upon leaving Phoenix. And she did feel, still, like Surfside was the home of her heart.

But also, she wondered if her heart had room to add a little more happiness. And if so, was it smart to see if Austin could help her heart bloom?

Chapter Eleven

After rinsing off Rainbow and stashing her on the cafe's board rack, Leyla checked through the Pier Three window. She'd come off the waves earlier than she would have normally, determined to enact her plan. Mostly because, if she didn't, she'd have to confess as much to Zora, and the rest of her day would be an entire text chain bouncing between nagging, pestering, and teasing.

She didn't have time for that.

She spied Austin through the cafe window, so she detoured back to her car long enough to wriggle out of her wet suit and grab their stuff. She wore his backpack on her shoulder when she walked in. Out of habit, she glanced at the end counter, but it was empty. She turned back to Austin, who'd been stock still until that second.

"One hazelnut latte, hang on." He activated his bustling mode, and over the hiss and whirr of the machines, she was left standing there wondering when, exactly, she'd gotten to expecting him to have prepared her usual drink while she was still outside tending to her board.

And also whether, for all those times she'd shrugged it off

as the same customer service he'd provide for anyone, she was totally deluding herself into accepting his special treatment as no big deal.

"Austin." She timed her statement to rise up in the gaps between coffee noises.

He paused with his hand on the frother, something unusually cool on his face when he looked to her. Maybe that flirtatious grin had been a special thing for her, too.

"When you have a sec, will you come chat?"

He'd nodded and finished up her drink, handing it to her directly instead of setting it on the pick-up counter. The brush of his fingers made hers tingle, and she dry swallowed to stop any shaking.

Whatever else her and Zora's plan was, she needed to set aside a little time to think about that tingle and what it meant.

When Austin joined her, she was trailing her fingers over his backpack straps again, of all nonsensical things. She shoved it across the table at him, so whatever strange temptation had her acting that way, she'd be unable to indulge it.

Austin looked simultaneously sunken in on himself and braced for a blow, and she knew she'd best speak fast or his sadboy eyes were gonna imprint themselves on her visual cortex.

"What I said in my apartment, you maybe could have interpreted. Wait, not maybe. You probably did interpret it as rejection."

He bit his lips together.

The crux of her plan involved speaking up, so she didn't let any uncertainty hang in the air. "It was not a rejection. I won't say I wasn't surprised. You were right about me not knowing what you'd been thinking—feeling—but that's me. So me being surprised? You can't just guess that means I'm unhappy about it."

She was outright glowering at him, and a man of sense

would take that to mean her face held more truth than her statement, but apparently Austin Wells was not a matter of sense.

His mouth spread wide, revealing that crooked canine, and he scooched closer. "So you're not unhappy, huh?" His knee brushed hers for a sec, and she found herself grinning right back at him.

"You're sitting there building entire castles from one statement, I can tell."

He shrugged. "One of my specialties. Does it make you unhappy if I do?"

She made a deliberate choice to tap her ankle against his calf. Something he couldn't misconstrue as a glancing bit of contact. "We'll get to talking about whether or not I'm happy another time. Right now you're on shift, and I want us to work out a couple of logistics before you get too pulled away by customers."

His smile was in his eyes and his cheeks and his goddamn hair, practically. Definitely also in his shoulders, and spreading down his arms to where his wrists rested on the table between them. "Got it. We're being serious people, focused and devoted to our agenda right now. I can roll with that."

His fingers were tapping one two three four / four three two one / one two three four against the pads of his thumbs, and damn if it wasn't cute to see him lift his shoulders up and back to settle them, and to nod oh so serious at her. "So, listen."

"Yeah?"

"Before I told you how much I am into you and then ran away. Maybe you remember this?"

She rolled her eyes.

"Oh good. I figured you would. You're smart. But, point is, we were talking about all the Expo work, and you came in with a full-on spreadsheet and stuff."

"You can say shit in front of me Austin. I'm not going to faint."

His turn to roll his eyes. "You came with a full-on fucking spreadsheet and shit, and all I contributed was a couple of line items. Maybe that's how you like to work. If so, I can completely respect that. I mean, I've known you for a good few years now and haven't ever found something I don't completely respect about you. But I learned my lesson about taking things as said. So, here I am articulating it. You've taken point on this, and if you want to keep on that way, I am yours to command."

He winked, which she thought about letting herself giggle over, and then decided he hadn't earned such a thing from her as of yet.

"So, my question: do you want us to keep on as we are? I'm down for that, but at the same time, if you want me to take more control, so you don't have to be the one thinking up all the next steps, or keeping track of the steps we've already thought up—you've already thought up—that's something we can do. No problem. I'm supposed to be learning how to manage projects as it is. But I won't step on your toes. You tell me how you want us to work."

Fuck, Austin, just hand over the keys to your entire soul while you're at it, why don't you?

He reached for his backpack as something to do with his fidgety fingers while he waited for her response, because the alternative was opening his mouth again and revealing even more of his increasingly not-secret yearnings for her. Just because she'd shown up today and said she wasn't completely opposed to his feelings, didn't mean she was going so far as to yearn in return.

She asked more about his classes, slipping into some kind of teacher/advisor zone.

He had to call a halt to that. "It's not that I don't appreciate the interest. I mean, my family's made it more than clear that I need all the advice and help I can get if I'm ever gonna get anywhere with my academics, but." He glanced around the coffee shop in a charade of noticing his job duties, but really it was about shaking off the sudden vision he'd had. Clear as the glassy green face of a barrel wave, he'd imagined his family knowing he was (finally) working towards his degree, and knowing he'd told Leyla he was interested in her.

They'd waste zero amounts of time suggesting that her studiousness and obvious plans for success were a perfect model for him. Any kind of questions or issues he had, they'd instantly advise him to seek out Leyla's counsel, and then reach out to her themselves, since they'd be sure he'd fuck up the ask.

After all, they were the primary people pointing out his pattern of fucking up his entire life.

His stomach churned at how much they'd tell him what a good influence Leyla was, and the relief they wouldn't even think to hide about having somebody out there to take him in hand and guide him to a life they deemed acceptable.

He found himself hunching over his backpack. Leyla tilted her head at him with an expression his mixed-up heart didn't know what to do with.

"Hey," she said, all gentle and tender and not in the least like she thought he was a sexy man worth knowing better. "I think I have a Pavlovian kind of reaction to sitting at this table across from someone with classwork in hand."

He scrubbed his hand across his hair and gripped the back of his neck. Her foot tapped his leg again, and he came up with a smile. "Too much tutoring?"

She nodded. "Exactly. Can't sit here with my hazelnut

latte and a student across from me without going into tutor mode. You didn't ask for that. I'm sure you don't need that."

He snorted. "Kind of you to suggest, but I wouldn't claim to have gotten myself entirely beyond the need for academic help. That's ... anyway Do you still do tutoring? I thought you were done was all that?"

"Well, yeah. I am. Weird to think it, but once I paid my last semester's tuition in January, I shut down that whole business."

God, Leyla's self-satisfied grin was infectious, even more so than her normal enchanting face. He offered her the fist bump she clearly deserved.

"Way to go. Tell me about stopping. Did you not like it?"

"Nah, it was fine, but I've been on that hustle for nearly eight years. Ever since I first surfed."

Head tilting, he asked, "Surfed? Really?"

"Yeah. You know my fam's all in Arizona, right?"

He nodded. "Weird, I never thought about how a desert girl like you got into surfing. I should have held more curiosity."

She shook her head. "No big. It's not much of a story. We used to drive down to the beach in Mexico for our vacations, and once I finally pestered my folks into getting us surf lessons —me and my sis—I was as hooked as I thought I would be. I wanted more access to the ocean. I knew our college funds would take care of in-state tuition, but." She shrugged. "Ain't no waves at Arizona State."

"I bet."

"So I knew I wanted to be where I could surf. And I knew I wanted to study something about ocean ecology. Wasn't long before I targeted Surfside as my dream school. My mom showed me my college savings, helped me do the math. We calculated out what I'd need so I could get my master's without going into scary debt, and I started my tutoring business the next day."

He almost needed to blink back tears at how fucking amazing she was. It was goddamn humbling to know more of how she'd developed and followed through on an attack plan to get where she was. He wasn't taking the graciousness of her offer to help lightly. "Thanks for sharing all that. But, what can we do to break the tutor pattern for us? You want to go for a walk on the beach, or down the pier? Or do we need a writing surface? The conference table's in use, but we could go sit in one of the studios. Or maybe you don't want to talk now. Here I am taking you for granted again. I'll scoot back to my counter, and you just text me let you know what you want."

Now she was the one looking back at the empty counter.

Oh, right, his job. "Alicia will be here in about twenty minutes if you have time to hang out."

She nodded and he blew out a breath. It was a trial to sit there across from her, entirely awkward and entirely unable to stop staring. Blessed customers arrived just then, giving him the excuse he needed to jump up and back away like the bunny rabbit he apparently was.

Leyla ducked her head to her coffee cup, and he decided it was to hide how she was charmed by him, instead of to conceal an expression of 'what the fuck am I getting myself deeper into?'

For the rest of his shift, he chanted to himself, "She's not sorry she kissed me she's here by choice she wants to talk more." His sister's knowing-ass look when he mentioned taking off early didn't begin to land on him, because he was floating, and no snark from Alicia would bring him back to earth.

Chapter Twelve

Leyla gathered herself up as Austin approached, only to stop short at his low moan. She checked him, and his cheeks were pomegranate red. Or what she assumed was pomegranate red, based on the color of the tinted lip balm she was applying. She rubbed her lips together and released them with a pop that wasn't so loud it drowned out another little moan.

He snatched up his backpack and held it in front of him, and Leyla absolutely did not release a throaty chuckle at the realization that he'd gone stiff watching her coat her lips.

She was hardly some siren, but it didn't take a ton of experience with turned-on guys for her to make an educated guess about what was crossing Austin's mind. *And what are you going to do about it?* She could practically hear her sister's teasing inquiry. It was a damn good question, and one she wasn't quite ready to answer. Instead, she tilted her chin towards the patio doors. "Pier?"

"Pier." He nodded and passed across another latte.

"Oh, I ..."

His smile went full charm buckets and his voice dripped innuendo. "It's on me."

The boy was charming. That's all there was to it.

He shouldered his backpack and plucked his own go-cup from the counter. It was one of the Pier Three reusable ones.

"I should get me one of those. Or a couple of them. I keep adding to the recycling burden."

"Well, first of all, all of our disposable cups are compostable. So, you shouldn't be adding to recycling or landfill either one."

"No lie?"

He shook his head. "Always have been, always will be. We care about the climate, too, even if we don't have your degrees. Second of all, you can absolutely drop a reusable mug on the outside sill when you're headed to surf. We bring them in and make whatever the order is when people are coming in off the waves."

"How do you know who wants what? Or does everybody always get the same thing, like me?" She sipped her, as usual, delicious hazelnut latte.

They made the zigzag that allowed them to mount the pier. "It's on our app. People place their order and upload a photo of the cup so we can match the drink to the vessel. They specify to have it ready in an hour or whatever looks right when they get to the beach or read the surf report."

"Fancy. Why didn't I know about all this?"

Because, she reminded herself, all this time she thought he was great at memorizing everyone's go-to order and getting them ready when they finished surfing. When instead, everyone else was using technology, and she was the only one relying on Austin to read her innermost desires.

Austin contented himself with a sip of his drink, checking out the lineup to their right as if he was trying to place the individual surfers out there.

"How come we never surf together?"

He turned to her. "We have."

"Not as an on-purpose thing, though. Only when we've happened to be out at the same time. Is it because you only like a longboard?" She almost always surfed with Rainbow, her gorgeous narrow-nosed fish board. She loved the fast take-offs and the way it let her carve through the mid-sections.

Her little student apartment didn't leave much room for her to add more to her quiver, but one of the stellar things about Noah's Surf Shop was his low rental rates for regulars, so she could grab a longboard on those days when the waves were weak but not mushy.

Austin shook his head. "I love cruising a zen ride as much as the next guy, but no. I'm a shortboard man at heart. I need the speed, you know? Though my newest stick is a seven-foot mini mal I'm liking the maneuvers on." He huffed a breath. "You should have seen the look of relief on my dad's face when my uncle Nathan—Noah's dad. He's the one who taught us all how to surf. Uncle Nathan told him I was ready to move to a shortboard and Dad was all, 'great, channel the boy's energy.' And I've not really looked back."

Her own folks had been less delighted with her move to faster rides and bigger waves. "Seriously?"

"Oh, yeah. We were coming up to the point where there weren't a lot more maintenance skills dad or Val—he was the super up at our complex my whole life, until he hit retirement. Anyway, he and Dad kept trying to come up with more things to teach me, because I'd get antsy doing the jobs that I already knew how to do. There was only so far they wanted to let me loose on the world with my set of baby's first power tools."

She laughed, imagining a little Austin running up and down the apartment hallways looking for something else to attack with his Fisher Price drill set.

"You get the picture." He nodded. "So, that was me, always looking for something else to learn. And putting me on a shortboard really did the trick of giving me something new to focus on."

She hummed. "I bet. How old were you?"

He shrugged. "Ten, eleven? Young enough I couldn't stick a board under my scrawny little arms and take the bus down here. Not that I was up for surfing this beach yet, but Uncle Nathan kept me in all the right places until I was sure-footed enough to come down here."

"Is that part of your ..." Lost for the right words, she gestured with her cup to the waves like he'd get it.

"Part of my what?"

"Your thing with channeling your energy into new projects. Seems like as soon as you finished building up Pier Three into a sustainable business, you went and built the studios, and now that's all in hand, you're working on the Expo. Is it a focus thing?"

His laugh was warm and, admittedly, a bit wonderful. "You don't have to think of a nice way to ask, Leyla. I don't think anybody I've met since I was maybe four has been unaware that I've got ADHD. The armchair diagnoses only outpaced the official one by a year or two."

She smiled. The straight-forwardness of his reply had the unexpected effect of making her feel closer to him.

They passed a trio packing up their fishing gear on the south-facing side of the pier and she drew him to the north edge, settling down with her feet hanging toward the water. They watched the last few surfers out there trying to make the most of the waves despite the incoming tide. Austin sat with his backpack between them. She took it and stacked it on top of her messenger bag, sliding closer.

"I think we should surf one morning together on purpose."

It didn't take Austin long to flip into flirtation mode. "Oh, yeah?" He shifted that bit more so their shoulders touched, letting his legs dangle beside hers. "For this hypothetical tandem surfing we're doing, it's dawn patrol, right?"

He was cheesing so much the fishers behind them were probably going to pull wheels of brie out of the Pacific instead of halibut or walleye.

She oozed some triple-cream right back at him. "Of course it's dawn patrol." Because it really was damn good to be on the waves as the sun climbed over the mountains that hugged their eastern horizon.

"So you know how some nights you're just like, damn, I really got to get to bed so I can get up in time for dawn patrol?" He said it like it was one of those global problems people spent decades of R&D to figure out.

She wasn't exactly pointing out that they both were well-established early risers, or that she rarely managed to stay awake past ten at night. No, she was playing along with the man, and wouldn't that make her sister stop and slow clap?

"It's a struggle," she said like she meant it. Like she wasn't the one bounding from room to room every Christmas morning, waking up every member of the household, even now in her late twenties.

He nodded his agreement. "So, if you think it would help, for convenience sake and all, we could grab an early dinner some night, then you could come sleep over at my place. That way, in the morning we'd be able to encourage each other to rise and shine."

If it weren't for the way the low morning sun edging over the foothills behind them cast brightness on his face, letting her see the shadow of uncertainty in his eyes, maybe she'd have stopped going along with Austin's cocksure-sounding nonsense. But, fact was, that one kiss in her apartment was intriguing enough she wanted to explore more of their flirtation. Hitching a leg up onto the dock, she shifted to face him, setting her coffee down and threading her fingers into his hair.

He snatched her waist and closed the distance, whispering her name with both glee and reverence just before their lips met.

He wasn't running away this time. Two times Leyla kisses him, and both times he's said up front what his intentions are?

For sure not letting her go.

No. Instead, Austin slid enough to brace one leg against the pier—last thing he wanted was either of them to land in the rocky foam below—and scooped Leyla closer. Hard as it was to fathom, even though she could do a thousand times better than him, she let him run his fingers up her spine to cradle the nape of her neck. Let him plant his other hand on her hip and squeeze as she opened to his explorations.

A hundred hazelnut lattes he'd made for her, and never suspected the way the sweetness of the brew would echo the creaminess inside her mouth. Lush. Heady. Perfect.

He was kissing Leyla on a sun-bright morning, and it was perfect.

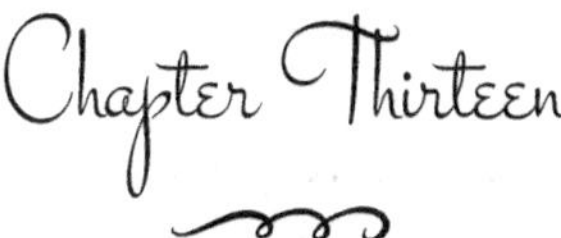

Chapter Thirteen

Okay, so she was getting super horny on the second busiest pier in town.

Not exactly like her, but since her normal MO struck her as kind of boring at that moment, she was happy to break the mold. Happy to try this new thing of getting hot and heavy with Austin before she'd even had breakfast.

It was something about the way he held her so firm, but his lips were so gentle. And the way his defined muscles rippled under the warm softness of his shirt. And the way the pier roughly scraped her calves while the Pacific breeze fluttered her hair.

It was all contrast after delicious contrast after delicious contrast. So she forced whatever thoughts she'd harbored about her too-predictable life to go stack themselves next to all her previous notions of how her day would go.

Zora would scoff at her and Sally would twist her lips knowingly. But even with all the evidence pointing this way, she hadn't fully believed in the inevitability of this moment. Of this kiss.

Some scientist she was, rejecting all those hypotheses

despite the accumulation of data. Time to start building whole new theories, with the help of empirical evidence like Austin's soft growl and his roving hands and the way her heart was accelerating like she didn't get excellent cardio workouts while surfing several mornings a week.

Her hand was crawling inside his shirt and up his abs when he pulled away. It took them both a few moments to steady their breathing, and if his blown pupils were anything to go by, Austin was as gobsmacked by their connection as she was.

He reached for her hands, drawing them off his skin, which, honestly? Rude. Her fingers wanted to explore his distinctly nice abs some more. She glared down at his hands, but instead of releasing her, he just laughed a little and squeezed her fingers. It somehow brought her round to the awareness that he was wearing a Pier Three Coffee shirt. Of course he was. Because he was still on shift.

"Hey." He rested his forehead against hers, grinning in a delightfully distracted way.

"Hey, yourself. So, you ready for that early dinner?" She matched him grin for grin.

"Pretty sure it's a little too early just yet."

"Spoilsport. You're the one who left his sister alone behind the counter and ran off."

He groaned. "Don't remind me. It'll be a long time before I hear the end of it."

"Complaining?"

He leaned in for another kiss. Regretfully brief, but incredibly emphatic. "Not a bit. This was worth every second of how much they're gonna tease me. But for real, when can we get together again? I do realize I was being a brat earlier, and you may not be at 'jump in bed with the guy who keeps panting after you' levels of interested in me. Yet."

"There you go, trying to talk yourself out of a good idea again."

He brought their joined hands to his chest, just over his heart. "You, Leyla Robinson, are definitely trying to torture me into admitting more things than—" He paused, then laughed. "Well, I guess there's not that much more I can admit than I've already done. So, fine. I'm at your disposal. An entirely open book full of desire for you. Are you free tonight?"

She didn't want him to be the only one putting himself out there, so she was the one who went in for a kiss, pressing their hands to her heart this time. "I am free tonight, but I definitely couldn't surf tomorrow. Rainbow and I have to wait until Saturday to get back out on the waves."

"So no sleepover until Friday?"

She shook her head. "Alas, no."

"And out of nothing but idle curiosity, did you tell Sally or Noah that you'd be at bonfire on Friday?"

She answered with a rueful laugh.

"Well, damn. Not that I mind. We can skip it, or we can show and listen to the inevitable commentary."

"There will be commentary," she agreed.

"Tell me about it." He disentangled their legs and stood, reaching to give her a hand up. "If this is a terrible idea, or if you're not comfortable, you'll feel free to renege?"

"Austin—what's your middle name?"

"Octavio."

"Octavio?"

"It's a Dad thing. He's into Roman history and all that. Abe is Abraham Augustus, after Caesar Augustus, the first emperor. And then Licie is Alicia Gaia, because Caesar Augustus was born Gaius Octavius Thurinus—stop me if I'm getting too Wikipedia on you. Dad really, really likes this guy. He was Julis Caesar's great-nephew and heir. So, yeah, that's how I ended up with Octavio. Personally, I think he should have looked into other historical figures. Austin Nefertiti has a ring to it, right? But instead we all got first names that start with A and middle names all after some guy who was literally ruling when Christ was born, so. That's me."

She snorted a little. "Right then, Austin Octavio Wells. Quit talking yourself out of things that we've already agreed on. We're skipping bonfire Friday night, and going out to dinner. Going back to your place and refusing to answer a single call or text from that entire crew until, I don't know. Monday or something."

His slightly feral crooked grin was back when he echoed, "Monday?"

They halted at the entrance to Pier Three. She returned his grin with a wicked expression of her own and winked. "Play your cards right. We'll see."

His shout of laughter trailed her exit and added buoyancy into her every step.

Friday morning, she was up early thinking about very little besides what to throw in a bag for her dinner and surfing date. Austin had offered up his shortboard or his thruster or any of the other sticks in his quiver, which he'd texted about seven pictures of. Supposedly so she could get a sense of what she wanted, but she suspected also so he could show off both the boards and his storage rack.

Whatever she picked, Rainbow could stay behind, but she still needed her wetsuit and her sleep bonnet and hell if she wasn't going to also pack the lacy white nighty Zora had sent her out of the blue a couple months back.

"The hell is this for?" she'd asked.

"You're super welcome," her sister had replied. "Thought

since you never seem to get some you could use all the help I could think up."

"Oh my God, you are the worst."

"I love you, too," Zora'd replied and then hung up on her. Brat. And never mind that this was the first time she'd found a use for the thing since then. After balancing standing on the toilet seat and twisty-turning to get some clue from her view in the mirror above the sink of how it looked on her, she packed the nightie, too. Finally organized, she hustled herself to the committee meeting.

Dean Tyler opened his wide, welcoming arms and waved her into the room like she was a rabbit he'd just pulled from his hat. She resisted, once again, the urge to tell him everything he thought he'd done for her was something she'd mapped out for herself long before they'd met.

She'd have a hell of a lot easier time thanking him for his part in her academic career if he'd quit acting like her whole life was his bright idea. Just as he was done parading her around the table introducing her to everyone else, the door opened, and who walked in but goddamned Chad. He sought her out first thing, circling his own way around the table and stopping to put a chummy hand on Dean Tyler's shoulder.

He jumped right in with his expostulations. "I can't thank you enough, sir, for inviting me to join this group. I'm honored to participate, knowing how essential it is to ensure that marginalized and disadvantaged people receive all the help they need to keep up with their academic careers."

He did not just say, 'keep up.' She narrowed her eyes. Never mind the apples and oranges parts of what they did; every single seminar she and Chad took together, he lagged behind not just her, but so many of the other students, histori- cally underrepresented or no. And never mind the gossip she'd heard from Jenni about his GRE scores and the skin of his teeth bachelor's degree.

She thought of Austin then. Everything he'd told her about his learning differences, and the way his family categorized him as unsuccessful because of his approach to higher education. Goddammit all to hell because she was in no mood to drop her intellectual snobbery about Chad, but now it felt borderline evil to hang on to it.

Still, he was going on about finding ways the university could compensate for incoming students from at-risk demographics, and he didn't even try hiding his smirk from her. So she'd ease up on her intellectual snobbery about Chad, fine, but that didn't extend to giving him credit for worming his way onto this committee and using it as a yet another platform utter a shit ton of barely veiled supremacist insinuations.

He could have as many difficulties with traditional education as Austin, but until he stopped treating the world like it owed him candy and riches just for existing, she wasn't changing her stance on what an entire tool he was.

She finally escaped the meeting and headed straight to the library to snag Sally's attention.

Her friend raised expectant brows, then lowered them in crease when she caught Leyla expression. "What?" She lowered her voice and looked around for the intern. "What's wrong?"

She followed Sally to the reference desk where they could sit and chat like she'd shown up for academic help instead of the need to rant and gnash her teeth. "Did something go wrong with the committee?"

"Chad was there."

"What?" Sally clapped her hand over her mouth and hunched towards her. "The fuck you mean Chad was there?"

"I don't know what he did to smooth talk Tyler, but the man invited him to join the group."

"Wait. He's actually on this committee?"

She nodded, grim. "He volunteered to be the secretary."

Sally's expression matched the disgust dripping from

Leyla's voice. "How's he gonna serve the mandate? Does he have one gram of expertise?"

Leyla scoffed. "You know damn well he doesn't. And he actually talked about how hard it will be to find counselors at low-performing high schools who would even care about any initiatives we came up with."

Sally's spine whipped straight up like she'd been slammed against a wall. She yanked the keyboard towards her and started typing.

"What are you doing?"

"I'm checking to see who else is on this committee."

"What for? Come on. It's fine. I mean, it sucks, but it's not like he can be that obstructive. And the whole point was for me to do something to get Tyler's quid pro quo for the Surfside Swell Expo."

"No." Sally was typing in her faster-than-thought way. "The point was for you to get the Expo without goddamn Chad finding out and turning it against you. If we can't get the Expo to work for this year, then we'll come back to it another time. Dunlavy's only got the one position this year, and I'll be damned if anything comes from this and costs you that job."

She leaned over and put a hand on Sally's forearm, not that it stopped her superhuman typing. "Babe, I didn't come here to get you to fix anything, okay? I just wanted to growl a little."

"Oh, I'm growling." Sally's bitter laugh was a little too loud for the library, at least according to the look the intern gave her as he wheeled his cart past them.

"Sally," he said.

"Derek," she clipped right back at him, and Leyla made a mental note to tease her friend more about all that later on.

Sally's sidelong glance promised she wasn't in the mood

for anything of the sort just then, which just made Leyla all the more determined, as her friend should know.

"Okay, hey. We agree Chad is evil and will try his best to undermine me by being a part of this. What's done is done. We can't change the fact he's sneaked his way in. And we can't change the fact he's going to try to turn it to his advantage. So, if there's anything to be done about it, and I'm not positive there is, I think it's just to be sure he doesn't find a way to make his advantage outrank mine in Dunlavy's view. And if Dunlavy is more swayed by Chad's presence on a committee to review the university's diversity action plan than they are by mine, that only speaks to bigger problems with the corporate culture than I'd feared."

Chapter Fourteen

Noah: Can we do that thing with the spiked coffee at bonfire tonight?

Austin: text Alicia. I'm not going to bonfire tonight

Noah: excuse me? not going to bonfire?

The number of emojis his cousin fired at him, you'd think it was the first time he was ever missing the Friday night event.

Austin: Don't worry. I'm sure you can talk A into bringing coffee. Plus, you can ask Mateo about the biscotti, which is all you really wanted in the first place

Noah waxed rhapsodic over the combination, which had become a bonfire staple back when Mateo and Alicia were first figuring out their relationship. Or maybe it was when they were still pretending to be just friends. He couldn't remember. Point was, just because Austin was the first person to bring spiked coffee to bonfire didn't mean he'd invented the concept. It had been a spur of the moment thing, in response to Alicia's very correct complaint that she'd become a de facto bonfire organizer, instead getting an equal chance to chill out with the rest of them. So, he'd shown up the next week with some thermoses of spiked coffee, and they'd all alternated bringing it periodically ever since.

He wasn't trying to make Alicia the default provider again. Her proximity to the beach wasn't an issue, now she'd moved in with Mateo, but he made sure she wasn't carrying the mental load, either. In this case, though, he and Abraham were both unavailable, so the baton had to go to her.

None of that stopped Noah from acting like Austin was denying him essential services. It wasn't even an especially cool night, so why his cousin needed spiked coffee instead of a beer he couldn't guess, unless it really was a biscotti addiction.

He went back to cleaning his place. There was more to do for his bathroom repair, but the prospect of Leyla spending the night had spurred him to finish hanging the sheetrock, texturing and painting the ceiling, and getting a primer coat on the walls. The room was still bland, and he'd end up needing to do touch up once the counters he ordered were in, but he wasn't inviting her to spend the night and requiring her to wander down to Callie's messy old apartment when she wanted to wash up.

Which reminded him to update his project wall with the note about the low-VOC flooring he'd ordered to finish up refurbishing 104, now he was done using the unit as his spare bathroom.

It didn't take long before his phone was ringing. He saw it was Noah and ignored. And ignored and ignored, until it was annoying to ignore the ringing while trying to lay a smooth link of caulk. When the next call came he slapped his hands dry against his jeans and answered. "What?"

"Hello to you, too."

That wasn't Noah, so he took a sec to check his screen. "Sally. What's up?"

He folded into a seat on the floor, closing his eyes so he

wouldn't keep looking at all the places his bathroom remodel was less than adequate for Leyla's visit.

"Noah says you're not coming to bonfire."

"Is there a law that I have to? Why are you even talking about it?"

She made one of those dismissive noises. "You know me and Noah are besties. We talk about everything."

"Why are you besties?" He really wasn't trying to derail Sally, but it occurred that he'd never heard their origin story, and was suddenly super curious.

"Oh, it was convenient."

"Convenient?"

"Yeah. We met when he started college, and you know how it is. Everybody going around working to redefine themselves on their own terms now that they're away from home and family."

He didn't know, actually, since college was less than three miles from his childhood home, and the majority of the people he knew there were from his high school and community. But the way Sally talked, it apparently was a common experience. So he agreed. "Right."

"Well, he'd just come out, you know, and—"

"But I thought everybody knew he was gay when he was like thirteen."

Her voice sounded like she was rolling her eyes at his obliviousness. Though in his defense, he'd been eight or nine when Noah was thirteen. "Maybe you knew when he was thirteen, but he hadn't told anybody. Your uncle and aunt or whatever. So there he was, a first year student, and there were these people in our dorm who were like, 'Oh, Noah, you're gay? Tell me your coming out story. Tell me your existential pain. Let me be the one you lean on.' Just prodding at him, demanding he share instead of giving him the space to do so if he wanted."

"He could have leaned on us." On him and his siblings, he meant.

"That's not the point. Point is, I walked into the common room once, and saw people poking at him like that, and his face was an entire storybook of not interested. So I went over and pulled him to me and we walked out. He was like,' Thanks, what's your name?' And I said, 'I'm Sally and I've decided. You be my gay best friend. I'll be your Black best friend. And then we have our bases covered and don't have to deal with shit like that back there.' And so that's how we've rolled ever since."

He thought on that for a bit. It seemed so easy: just walking up to somebody and announcing a friendship. He'd tried something similar back in grade school and it hadn't been all that successful. In retrospect, his grade school self was hardly the most regulated of kids, which might have made his friendship offer unappealing. At any rate, he'd given up on trying to make friends that way, drifting eventually to glomming onto his sibling's friend groups, and otherwise, just aiming to be entertaining and useful when he met people like Ty or Isaac. Those guys, if not exactly friends, at least were close enough to be called buddies.

"I'm not gay or Black, but do you want to be my friend, too?" There went his brain blurting shit out without permission again.

She laughed. Sally was kind, so probably she wasn't laughing to attack him.

He waited. Went back to staring at the join between the bathroom's ceiling and wall, wondering if he should tack up the ceiling molding now. It would give the room a cleaner look before Leyla arrived. But would it cost him too much time, between pulling out his miter box, cutting the sticks to length, cleaning up the sawdust?

Probably it wasn't the best use of the time he had until meeting Leyla for dinner.

"We're already friends, Austin," Sally was saying.

He blinked. "We are?"

She scoffed. "Well, I thought we were but ..."

"Yeah, absolutely. We are. I'm happy we are. I guess I just didn't know for sure."

"Austin, we hang out nearly every week and you're obsessed with my best friend."

"I'm not obsessed with Noah."

"With my female best friend."

"Isn't it reductive to categorize best friendness by demographics?"

"Patience of a saint, that's what I have," Sally muttered. She cleared her throat. "I'm a librarian. I categorize. It's what I do. And Noah and Leyla know perfectly well how much I treasure them both."

"Then why did Noah make you call me today? Does he think it's a bad idea for Leyla to date me?"

"Noah doesn't know that's why you're not going to bonfire tonight."

"He doesn't?"

"Unless you told him?"

"No, but ..."

"Austin, listen."

"He was complaining about the biscotti thing, but I didn't tell him."

"Austin."

He clamped his mouth shut and listened.

"I know you and Leyla are going out tonight instead of to bonfire. And when Noah started complaining to me ..."

"He can just ask Mateo himself for the biscotti."

"That's not my point, Austin. When Noah started

complaining to me, first of all, I told him to order his biscotti directly from Mateo instead of counting on you to do it."

"That's what I'm saying."

"And second of all, I realized he doesn't know about your date plans. Because if he knew that's why you're missing bonfire, he'd hush about the biscotti."

"So he doesn't mind that I'm dating his best friend's best friend?"

"Nobody minds. I think it's about time you two went out. You've been gone over her as long as I've known you."

"Well, but ..."

"My point is, as your friend, Austin ..."

He smiled at that, because he thought she was going to give him shit about it for a century, and he looked forward to it.

"I know that you might have not told Noah out of a sense of keeping things private, since this is your first official date at all."

"Should I keep things private? Does she want to keep things private?" Oh god, what if she wanted to keep things private? Was that okay? It was Leyla; he'd take what he could get, so of course it was okay. But should he have thoughts about it?

"Austin," Sally said, recalling him to the conversation. "If she wanted to date you on the low, she'd have said. She didn't, which is why I thought I should check in with you to see what you want, before I spilled your business to Noah."

"It's Leyla's business."

"It's Leyla's and your business. You can have your own ideas about what's up for discussion around the bonfire."

"Like no one's gonna draw conclusions when she and I both are absent."

"Well, speculation isn't knowledge."

"Okay, librarian."

"Now you're getting it. So: I'm telling Noah, or I'm not telling Noah? I'm trying to let you know I'll keep your secrets."

"It's not a secret."

"Okay, that's what I wanted to know." Sally sounded approving. Her teasing tone dropped and her voice got warmer. "Just wanted to make sure you were cool with it."

"It's not the gossip or the teasing," he said, suddenly determined that one person—this certified friend of his—understand him a bit more. "Everyone's been doing that forever. Leyla is the only one who believed all the jokes weren't entirely based in reality."

"Like I didn't tell her over and over again."

His cheeks were warm but he ignored that. "I just know once everyone knows we're ..." He trailed off because his throat closed tight at the very precipice of naming the thing he wanted for so long.

"In a relationship, dating, seeing each other?"

He swallowed past the rusty lump of fearful denials. "Anything along those lines, yeah. Cause they've—you and everyone else—have been telling her how I'm into her, but it was always more abstract, you know? Once they know she's agreed to date me, even if it's just this once ..." There went his throat rusting over again. "That's when it'll all ramp up on her, too. She doesn't need to be teased about me every time she shows up to grab a latte or hang out with your best friend."

"Austin." Now Sally sounded as warm and tender as his Dad sometimes did when letting him know he was not as useless as he'd feared. "We can talk about this, but I'm pretty sure Leyla is fully cognizant of the potential for teasing she's opened herself up to. She's been part of our group as long as anyone. Nothing about our dynamics has escaped her, I promise you that."

"She managed to not understand how serious I was about

her all this time." Ah, shit, that rusty lump had migrated straight to his heart, and if that wasn't a sign that he was harboring a little resentment about not being understood all this time ... He rubbed circles on his chest and worked on swallowing that down, because that was a him issue, not a somebody else issue.

"Just because she acted like she didn't know the score, doesn't mean she didn't know the score, Baby. Sometimes, and this is something you might reflect on yourself, people allow themselves to be unaware of certain truths so long as it suits their needs for wherever they are at that moment."

Sally let him digest those soothing words on top of the creaking grinding lump in his stomach, and then she burst out laughing. "Okay. I'd better hang up now. I texted Noah and he has things to say. I'm gonna try to intercept him myself so you can get on with preparing for your date."

"Ha. Good luck. And thanks for calling, and for ..." His hand traced over his heart again. "For all that you said."

She disconnected, leaving Austin to take stock of all the ways he felt just a little bit less alone.

Chapter Fifteen

She gave him some dining options, and he picked Lucille's. Not only because Lucille's daughter Sydney would likely be there to see they got a nice table and good service. As far as he could tell, all the waiters at Lucille's were great servers. It was something he and Sydney had talked about, back when they were going through precarious times and both wanted to ensure their staffs were well supported against asshole customers. That, and other ways to engender a supportive work environment. They both wanted to keep management on the side of their workers above all else.

It was Sydney who'd turned him on to the problem with peak time scheduling. After that, for the first time, he took a look at his shift schedules to be sure he wasn't asking anybody to close one night and open the next morning, leaving barely enough time in between to get a decent amount of sleep. Much less attend to all the non-work related demands of life.

Meanwhile, he brought her in on the discussions about a childcare co-op that focused on the needs of service workers who required unregulated drop-ins and second shift opening hours.

He ran his mind back through several of their past encounters and it felt like something cozy and warm had settled over his shoulders. "I'll text Sydney to see if she can't put our name down for a table now. I know it's early, but Lucille's stays busy from happy hour onward."

"Sydney is who, exactly?"

"Lucille's daughter." His smile grew. He was really going to have to thank Sally for clearing up some stuff for him. "She's my friend. She's been managing the restaurant for a couple of years now."

Sydney texted back. Oh *hell*, yes.

"What's that grin for?"

Sydney's cousin Dante was the chef, and he was the other reason Austin picked Lucille's over the other places. "Special tonight is fenugreek braised short-ribs."

Leyla groaned. "Put it in my mouth."

He started the car, but had to lean over and kiss that mouth before they got going. "One hundred percent my evil plan right there."

He got them to Lucille's without incident, even though as soon as they hit the road, Leyla's hand came to rest on his thigh.

She was so entirely fun, and he was so entirely thrilled about it.

Sydney didn't disappoint, coming out from the office to greet him with a cheek kiss, and ushering them to what she told the host was table eighteen. Before they could think about it, a waiter showed up with cocktails and a small tureen of baked okra, which they inhaled without delay.

Ditto with everything else that came to the table. The night was all eating and talking and Sydney showing up to chat a bit in case they felt even the slightest bit of one-on-one awkwardness. Not that he knew if Leyla felt any awkwardness. She wasn't acting any kind of notably different way towards him, but all day he'd been jumpy and fidgety enough that even he noticed it.

The aftermath of the phone call with Sally spiraled him tighter, and the moment Leyla handed him her bag to stash in the cargo area, he felt wound nearly to the snapping point. He had to keep checking to be sure his leg wasn't jiggling table eighteen, which, fortunately, rested on a very sturdy pedestal.

Another thing he needed to thank Sydney for, along with the swift service, the comped apps, and the time he was about to swallow his tongue watching Leyla slurp down an oyster and Sydney's question about scheduling their interview for the Expo podcast distracted him from lunging across the table and making an embarrassing spectacle of himself.

"No, I'm too stuffed," Leyla protested when the server mentioned desert.

"Even for bread pudding with a bourbon sauce?" the waiter asked, and never mind that that was the most innocuous, most typical kind of question ever asked. Something about it made Leyla catch his eye, and both started to laugh.

She licked her lips, and that was all instruction Austin needed. "Will you box that for us to go?" He handed over his credit card.

"You got it."

Austin relished the way Leyla exhibited her impatience as they waved to Dante in the kitchen and hugged Sydney goodbye and got their horny asses to his car.

"Know something?" she said, as he reached back to settle the dessert in the floor space behind him.

"What's that?"

"It's been an unacceptable number of years since I made out with anybody in a car."

"Oh yeah?"

She took ahold of his shoulder, stopping him from settling into the driver's seat. Not that he was in any hurry to be away from her personal space. It was exactly the only place he wanted to be. His next task was to find out if she was sure she wanted to come home with him, so he wasn't gonna risk missing out on her kiss, in case the answer was no.

He hoped the answer wasn't no.

Every indication was in his favor. But she was Leyla Robinson, sitting there gorgeous in her complicated knotted bronze top and those delicious black jeans, and he was only Austin Wells.

And he was going to explode or collapse or some sort of dire thing if it was more than a second more before he got to taste the sweetness of her skin.

Chapter Sixteen

She'd nearly hung up on Sally when the woman called to tell her how, in her opinion, Austin was a cinnamon roll disguised as a Casanova. Instead, she'd cut her off, but only after pointing out that if they were offering unsolicited advice, she had some comments about the Derek the intern.

"He's an intern," Sally said, which was what Sally always said.

Didn't matter if she was right. It was still only one facet of the dynamic between the two of them.

Next time it came up, she was going to point out how all of Sally's protests about their relative positions had gone from being dismissive, to outraged, and were now verging on petulant territory.

But even after disconnecting from her friend, it seemed like she was bound to have bits of Sally's appraisal floating across her mind during dinner. And after, too.

She was all caught up in Austin's sweetness, and how he went out of his way to give credit where it was due whenever he talked about his own endeavors, and the realization that now she'd opened herself up to the attraction between them, she could see all the ways he kept his focus on her no matter what was happening around them.

Plus, he was really fucking cute. Like, an exasperating amount of cute. Big sweet eyes and his hands—Sally had gotten ribald about how he was a handyman, and she pretended to shut that down, but: yeah, those hands.

They looked handy.

Throughout the meal—delicious but decidedly too long —those hands kept moving, constantly reaching towards her in a teasing dance that left her itchy for more. For real contact.

And now they were alone, and his hands—callused, assured, and attuned to her—landed on her body.

It'd been admittedly too long since she'd gotten intimate. Mostly due to her own lack of desire to bother, when she was a busy woman and bothering took effort. Besides, her schedule had been packed, and she'd liked spending her free time surfing and going to bonfire and hanging out with her friends.

Maybe also some part of her had liked that the hanging out meant being near the constant undercurrent of Austin's flirtation and charm. Even if it did take her being told directly he was horny for her before she faced up to it.

But now. Now she had time, and now she had Austin's hands on her body. All that teasing about him being handy? Not one single lie detected.

They were both breathing hard when they pulled apart.

"Good God, Leyla." His expression was half wonder and half glare.

"Me?" She laughed. "You're the one with ..." It probably didn't make sense, the way she waved her hands at his torso. But facts are facts, and fact was, he'd blown her heart into smithereens with the intensity of their parking lot kiss.

He dropped back against his seat. "Too much?"

Before he could untangle their fingers, she squeezed. "A lot. But not too much."

Slowly, his drew in a breath and swiveled his head to look fully at her. She was maybe a mess—shirt askew, lip gloss disappeared, braid out frizzed everywhere. Didn't seem like that bothered him, from the way his blown pupils stayed fixed and intent on her.

"I keep forgetting to ask if you're sure you want to go back to my place."

Her own breath hitched at the sweet determination he displayed. Always trying to do things right, that was Austin. Always sure he wouldn't succeed, too, or at least that if he did it was some kind of fluke. She wasn't the one to fix his self-doubt, she knew that. Didn't mean she wasn't going to make her own part in their dynamic sure enough that he could draw his own conclusions.

His hand was warm and firm in hers as she canted a bit more his way. She balanced her elbow on the console and shifted their fingers to a spot real high on his thigh.

His sharp gasp sent shivers coiling within her.

Leaving his hand behind, Leyla sent hers questing higher. Her touch was light and playful, but she made sure there was no mistaking her intent. Because she wanted this—wanted him—and because she needed him to know exactly how sure she was about their next stop.

"Take me, Austin." She followed her breathy statement with a gentle suck just below his ear. His cock twitched, hard already, and she rubbed her knuckles up his denim-clad length. "Take me to your place, and take me to your bed."

He wouldn't swear it was legal to drive with a distraction like Leyla Robinson in the passenger seat. Certainly not Leyla Robinson with her fingers toying with his dick, and looking all mussed and debauched from when she'd allowed his hands to roam her perfect body and his mouth to taste her perfect skin.

But she'd said yes. And yes was what he needed from her, and yes is what she claimed she wanted, so he stuck the car in drive and kept his hands at ten and two the whole way home. It was all he could do to grab her bags and escort her inside before his feral body took control of the situation.

They made it into his apartment and he just ... stopped. Stood poised, staring at her as she leaned against the back of his couch.

"Can I ...?" What the fuck was he even trying to say? He palmed his aching cock, transfixed by the jut of her breasts against her top. He couldn't come up with words other than *nipple*. And he wasn't sure saying that over and over again would plead his case.

He ripped off his shirt and stepped to her. And her hands were on him. And he sank his hips to hers, eager for contact. "Tell me no?"

She pinched his nipples, and he moaned. "And if I don't?" she asked, and did some sort of full body gyration that slid her torso all up and down his.

"Bedroom," he said, because he was fucking running out of words. Every one he could think up was cruder than the next, and she was going along with it. She was touching him. Her hips to his as he backed down the hall. Her whole body canted to him as they slid and they stumbled and they tumbled to his mattress and then—oh fuck—and then Leyla whipped her own shirt off.

And he was under like a riptide, because she was unfastening his jeans and then her own. And her bra was black with grey tracings of flowers across the cups, and her panties ....

He'd seen her in a bikini top with her wetsuit hanging around her hips. He'd seen her in shorts and tank tops. He'd seen her in sundresses. But Leyla Robinson in her black and gray bra with just the lacy top of her black panties visible was more erotic than any sight of his life.

She didn't seem to mind the way he gawped at her body, just did her own exploration of his. As if he anything comparable to offer. He wasn't ignorant of his own charms. Enough teasing and pleasure and sensation littered the background of his life for him to own that he was an attractive sexual partner, but all that meant was he could comfortably offer a skill level she deserved in bed.

It didn't mean that he had what it would take to bring Leyla happiness outside of bed. Her roving hands and her kisses and her smiles proved she was content with this, though. With who he was when they stripped down together. He wasn't foolish enough to turn down the opportunity. Not when she was tugging at his pants and his hips were dancing like they'd already gotten to the final act of this seductive play.

"Need to taste you. Is that all right?" Nude, his body as open to her as his heart, he shifted to the end of the bed so he could assist with the removal of her jeans.

"Mmm," she said, which wasn't no, and therefore seemed like an enthusiastic yes to him.

"If you—"

"Austin, if you give me one more out instead of eating me out right now I will storm naked down the hallway and pound on the neighbor's door until they let me in and call me a ride."

Yeah, that was fucking enthusiastic. He dipped his head and spread her thighs and finally, finally inhaled the blissful, heart-searing musk of her most intimate self.

His groan was half relief, half agony, and a thousand percent bliss, because Leyla tasted like low tide and the rising sun and sweat laced with foam.

He was intoxicated.

Giddy and gone.

Everyone teased how he'd been gone for her since the first

day she walked into Pier Three, and they weren't wrong, but that was so, so mild compared to what he experienced now. His entire concept of tranquillity changed the moment his head dove between Leyla's thighs.

Comparisons with unworthy, the past eradicated, but he knew immediately there was a vast difference between this moment and any second with any other lover.

He was anchored in a moment he would remember forever.

Chapter Seventeen

The man's tongue.

His rough but tender, all-knowing fingers. And his tongue.

And the noises? Who got turned on by the snuffling slurping satisfied noises of a dude at her core? Leyla, that's who. Or so she discovered, because each groan and growl bowed her higher and higher into tension and that triumphant sort of joy that comes with knowing any amount of effort and striving was gonna be worth it, that the payoff was inches away, that just in a moment, a few seconds more—one second, two seconds, maybe three—she would pop over the edge and sail into something explosively magical and turbulent and fun.

"Austin. Oh damn, yes. Austin." Her words were all affirmations and curses and his name and his name and joy.

"Hmm?" His head was still planted in heaven, and it took her a sec to realize that might be because of her insistent grip on his hair. She let up, smoothing and patting at his locks, but all that seemed to do was encourage him to deepen his explorations.

Well, who was she to fight a good idea? The second orgasm

hit fast, like it'd been just sitting back waiting for her to notice it was time to tumble.

When he looked up, he was smug as hell. Fair enough; so was she. That red flush traveled from his cheeks all down his neck and across his chest. She reached for his chin and dragged him to rise over her, so she could see exactly how rosy his skin got when he was turned on and, if she was right, bordering on desperation.

Yeah. Desperate. Leyla sidled out from under Austin and he collapsed to the mattress, grinning. One hand stroked her hip, the other his cock.

"Think you're something special, don't you?"

He jutted his pelvis in reply. And hell if he wasn't right, because despite the excellent orgasms she'd already relished, Leyla's whole self sent up an urgent need for him to be inside her. The glee in his eyes as she glanced towards his side table spoke volumes.

"Other one." He nodded to the opposite wall, and she kneeled up to reach where he indicated. It was then she noticed she was stretching over a satin-cased pillow.

"What's this?"

Even his ears went red then. Fucking adorable. "To protect your hair. Is it okay?"

"Hmph. And what if I like sleeping on the right side of the bed?"

Another thing about Austin was, his laugh filled the room. Even grabbing her around the waist and flipping them so her head landed on the silky pillowcase didn't take away from the power of his laugh. "Well, that's the deal-breaker. Sorry. If you can't let me sleep closer to the door, you may as well go home now. Want me to text my neighbor a heads-up about you pestering them for a Lyft?"

Since he'd managed to end up crouched over her with his breath tickling over her chest, she opted to shush his silliness by pinching her nipples into aching points. It did the trick. He lavished attention on her breasts, all his clever tongue tricks translating just great to each new erogenous zone he encountered. Leyla arched into him, hands roaming over his back, his sides, his ass.

And then her mind cleared enough to remember the condom. She felt like she was fumbling in absolute darkness, like it would take hours and decades until she got the damn thing open, until she captured his cock and rolled the latex down his hot length. It was seconds, not hours, but her sudden desperation matched—or maybe exceeded—what she'd seen in his blown-wide, deep brown eyes.

Damn him, Austin made his way to her mouth instead of thrusting in. Kissed her sweet and deep and long and heady with her scent overlaid on his spice-salt taste.

Pulled back and waited until she looked at him. "You're sure?"

Leyla never thought she was prone to violence before, but so help her, if Austin's cock wasn't sheathed in her immediately ...

Her laughing growl of affirmation, or maybe her death glare, or maybe the fact that she'd consented over and damn over again, finally seemed to penetrate. Because: penetration. She and he groaned together, all half-curse and half-nonsense. His flexed his pelvis, and again, each movement taut through his ass as she held him close. She wanted to always be holding his ass as he pumped into her. She wanted to starfish in abandonment as he moved over her. She wanted to undulate above him as his rough touch held her thighs wide.

That. That last one.

She wanted that.

One pinch to his taut ass and one kiss to his shoulder, and he knew somehow? A mystery she'd investigate later, because maybe she'd said it aloud in all her happy babble, or maybe he was the best body language reader in the universe, but all that mattered was how he supported her hips while they shifted. His torso spread below her, knees propped up to bolster her and give purchase to his thrusts. His fingers running along the crease of her hips and tickle-toying in dips and scrapes to her sensitive inner thighs.

And then he stared straight up at her, and bit his lip, and said her name.

Leyla moved, and Austin moved, and the wave of her body crashed into the wave of his. They smashed together, and she'd never been so full. She'd never felt every single bit of the slide and swivel of a cock as she clasped it in her core. She'd never breathed with the same intensity of her lover, knowing how he would move and him knowing where to touch, and seen the moment he determined to make her come again before he allowed himself the same pleasure.

His thumb tapped the sensitive hood of her clit. He licked his lip and thrummed her swollen labia, and she bore down on him, squeezing and rocking into his clever hold. And maybe he meant to wait, but Leyla had her own ideas. As she tilted into another orgasm, she plucked at his nipples and called his name and ground her pussy to surround him, and the wave of his passion kept her in the flow of her own while they moved and came and moaned and came together.

When they came to get ready for bed, he hardly even gave thought to whether his bathroom was tidy enough for her. He'd gotten too full up on good food and good sex and good conversation with Leyla to make room for intrusive worries.

Seemed like maybe he was hitting on a plan for the best way to bypass his brain weasels for the rest of his life: just be a thousand percent full of everything Leyla and he'd have no room left for worries.

She came out of the bathroom with her hair in some kind of high up thing she called a pineapple and went to her bag. He'd set it up atop his dresser after shoving aside all the supplies he used for his organizing, leaving her plenty of room to spread out as she liked.

She pulled out a bonnet and started to wrap her hair, and it turned out his weasels were perfectly happy to wriggle around in his brain even when he was completely full of Leyla.

"Um, is the pillowcase not right?"

She side-eyed him and he went up in well-deserved flames, because who was he to act like he knew better than she did what she'd need for her own hair?

"Sorry. I am what you might consider a little invested in the idea of you sleeping over more." She gave him another side-eye and he hastily added, "If that's what you want, of course. I understand if you're one and done with me. I'll even call the Lyft myself so you don't have to beg the neighbors."

The gesturing flair of her hand gave him permission he readily accepted to admire her frilly nightie. "No call for you to bug the neighbors. I've every intention of sleeping on that satin pillowcase. But one thing I've learned about you in the past couple hours is that you're a bit of a hair grabber."

Now he looked aslant at her, because his scalp was decidedly tender from her grip.

She came in for a kiss. "If you're up for me waking you in the middle of the night, or for you waking me? Either one of which I fully support, by the way. I'm making sure I don't have to spend an hour tomorrow putting my hair up in a protective style when it's time for dawn patrol."

He snatched her around the waist and spun them in a clumsy goofy dance. "I forgot to tell you—that's what your taste like."

"What is?"

"Dawn patrol. You taste like dawn patrol. All sunrise and salty and a bit of sweat and the day getting warmer."

She collapsed her head to his shoulder, torso shaking. It went on for way too many wordless moments.

He gulped and cleared his throat. "Shit, is that—are you …? You saw my car keys in the kitchen, right? You can just grab them and drive yourself home. You don't need to wait on a Lyft at all."

"You have to know that is the most ridiculous thing I've ever heard." She barely managed to speak her accusation through her laughter.

His hands relaxed enough to curl gently around her powerful sweet arms. "Why? It's the truth."

"You some kind of pussy poet now? I've never heard of dawn patrol as a flavor."

"No? Well, I'm right. Maybe you should take a taste yourself."

She snorted. "What makes you think I haven't tasted myself?"

His dick jumped at that, and she smoothed her hand down to squeeze his ass. "And, no, I don't just mean on your lips. I'm a grown-ass woman, Austin. You think I've never decided to sample my own juices?"

"Oh, hell. Did you really want me to wait until the middle of the night to have you again, or can we get back to it right now?" He was straining out of his boxers just from listening to her talk.

This time, Leyla was the one to back to them to the bed, muttering, "Dawn patrol," but not seeming to mind in the least when he set to work to confirm his hypothesis.

Chapter Eighteen

His groan woke her.

It wasn't the fun kind of groan, like he was buried deep inside her and listening to her dirty talk.

She croaked into her pillow. "What?"

"I thought you were a morning person."

She rolled over enough to eyeball him. The low light didn't stop her from catching the teasing glint in his eye. "Waking up early doesn't mean I'm sunshine first thing. Why do you think I stagger in for my coffee as soon as I get off the waves?"

"Mmm. Hold that thought." He tossed off the cover and hopped up like his muscles were on springs. That, plus some particularly flexible side-plank type stuff he'd done when they were fucking face-to-face in the night, his leg hitched over her waist for leverage as they moved so gentle and so intent ... yeah. It spoke to the yoga mats in his living room being more than props.

She was still playing scenarios in her head when he returned to the room, passing over a cold thermos before tugging on board shorts and a rash guard. "You have a wicked look in your eyes. I like it."

"What's this?"

"Iced latte. Hazelnut. What had you looking so devilish?"

The drink was everything she loved, except for not being hot. "Imagining you doing naked yoga. Why did you groan?"

He collapsed to the mattress, so it was a good thing the thermos had one of those auto-close drink spouts. "Cause you're thinking about me doing naked things."

She nudged him. "Not that. When you woke me up."

"Oh." He stretched back to snag his phone. "I turned my phone on to check the surf report—it's a little loose out, you want to take out the longboards?"

"Damn. I was hoping for fast water. I wanted to put your mini mal through its paces."

"Chance to prove to you I got tricks this way, though."

She set the latte on the bedside table and pinned him with a kiss. "I know you got tricks."

"Do my best. For you." He nuzzled her neck. "I do my best for you."

Before his hands got too exploratory, she scooted away. "Okay, Dawn Patrol, keep on with your story. In a sec."

When she returned from the bathroom, he'd somehow conjured up a couple of the energy muffins they sold at Pier Three, and a bowl of orange slices. She thanked him with a kiss and went to pull on her bikini and wetsuit.

"You haven't checked your phone?"

"If you think you're heading out to the water in just shorts, I will. I know it's got to be cold enough out there for a suit. Other day I was regretting not getting that 4/3 I've been eyeing."

"Ah, baby, come here, I'll keep you warm." His arms wide, his grin wider. Brat.

"It's too damn early in the morning for that cheese. You going to suit up or what? And what was on your phone?"

He whipped off the rash guard and handed over his cell. "Your bestie and my cousin think they're funny." Leaving her to read the new group text they'd created and named 'Austin finally makes a move,' he went to rummage in his closet.

After absorbing all of the nonsense—an incessant collection of short videos with Sally and Noah mock-interviewing everyone around the bonfire about what they thought Leyla and Austin were doing "at this very second," interspersed with articles about safe sex, consent, and various proclivities—she echoed his early morning groan.

"I told them. Well, I told Sally, anyway, that I'd been flipping a little because I didn't want you to come in for all the jokes I always get about you. That's why I didn't scream from the rooftops about our date. In case you thought there was more to it. Sally told me you knew what you were getting yourself into by agreeing to spend the night with me." His tone clearly conveyed he felt he was right to be skeptical.

Wordlessly, she passed back his phone and nudged him to the threshold of his own room. It felt proprietary, doing that, even more so when he just took her direction and leaned against the hallway to don a spring suit. She'd roll her eyes about that later. At least it had a hood.

She unlocked her own phone, changed the group text name to 'Leyla moves right back' and took a video of the room, zooming in on the twisted sheets, the tossed-aside blanket, the satin pillowcase. Finally, she pivoted to where Austin leaned in the doorway, a half-grin and messy hair and stubble she'd gotten real familiar with in the night.

"Hey, Austin?"

"Hey, Leyla?"

"What do you suppose you and I are doing at this *very* second?"

He licked his lips. She cut off the video in the midst of her shout of laughter, and hit send.

Fueled by Austin's breakfast, she found herself being downright chatty on the way to the waves. He'd asked her a hundred questions about her capstone project and her MS cohort over dinner. Now he wanted to know if there was a rivalry of any kind between the coastal scientists focused on the climate and those folks focused on fisheries. It was a starker division in his mind than in reality, though she got how he would view them in that kind of binary.

"No, we're all doing the same things, even if some of us are working on manta rays or steelheads or salmonids, while others are more about reef management or community-based conservation or sediment influxes or kelp restoration."

"Or ocean-based carbon dioxide removal pathways."

"Oh, somebody has been listening to me." She grinned around another sip of her cold latte.

"It's not every day I find out about how algae in cattle feed can reduce methane emissions across the country."

She felt her cheeks heat and shot him a look. He was positively laconic when he shrugged in return. "I don't have many ideas about how to save the planet myself. So when somebody shares her big brain knowledge, I'm gonna pay attention. And maybe set about doing what I can to support her."

All this sweet attentiveness of his was gonna have her reevaluating the way she thought about her work. Not that she would be any more dedicated to finishing her capstone and getting that Dunlavy job offer. But it'd been good minute since she had anybody listening to her describe her work with fresh ears. It made her want to devote a full day to describing her research. And at the same time, spend the whole day paddling out to mack the waves with Austin. To spin on the rails of his three-fin board and dance on the nose. To see him cruising the lines hanging ten, if he planned to show off as much as she suspected.

They were sitting back in the lineup, waiting for promising swell, when he paddled closer. "Okay I don't know about this, because it's your expertise, but. You know how were talking about developing incentives for the cattle feed thing?"

She nodded.

"Have you—probably you've thought of this."

She was about to pull him closer and remind him that sound didn't carry so perfectly in the coastal breeze, when some jake propelled his shortboard between them, snaking not just them, but the couple of guys lined up closer to the incoming swell. He then tried to pop up on an ankle biter and was immediately spat out in the foam.

A chuckle went up and down the line, the guy to her right muttering, "Quimby."

She turned back to Austin to share an eye roll, and then looked further. Tilting her chin at the set, she bounced a little. "Finally, something a little racy."

His face lit like the sun peeping over the foothills. "I love it when I find something worth waiting for."

Hard to tell over the crash of ocean, but she didn't think she'd be all wrong if she read some double meaning into his words.

Chapter Nineteen

An hour or so later they'd made their way across the beach to Pier Three. Austin led her up to the recording suite, which still held the full bath that had been Alicia's when the space was her apartment.

"We're locked in, and nobody's booked this morning," he said, handing over her bag. "If you want to shower, or just have some wiggle room while you change?"

"Do you want to shower?"

Even through the wind-roughened color on his face, she could make out his blush. "I can just rinse in the gray water outside. I'll be fine."

"Or ..." She turned so he could unzip her wetsuit.

He was behind her in an instant. "I like the way you're thinking. I didn't bring any condoms, though."

"You think I went and spent the night in some guy's apartment without packing my own protection? Just because we didn't use it, doesn't mean I don't have it."

"Some guy? That's me? Just some guy?"

She hummed her teasing reinforcement of that assessment.

"Pity he's not someone a little special to you or anything."

"Wow, look at you making assumptions all of a sudden."

He took a half step back and she turned to draw him close again. "I never said that was a bad thing."

He touched their foreheads together, which she was already coming to realize was a sign of strong emotion in him. "You are nothing but a danger to me, Leyla Robinson." Then he moved to nipping his way down her neck, which was a strong signal in itself, but of a lewder nature.

"You have a real funny way of lodging your complaints," she returned, following his lead to the bathroom. Before getting down to business, she dug through her bag. She'd packed enough of her toolkit to restore her braid out after surfing, and it would serve to get her in and out of the shower as well.

Glancing at the door—checking it would lock before fully committing to this plan that would leave her naked and distracted directly above a busy cafe—she bit her lip and regarded Austin under her lashes. Attracted as she was to this man and his constant stream of wicked sexy ideas, she was still her same cautious self at heart.

Plus, if something embarrassing was gonna happen, she would obviously tell her sister. And then she'd hear about it for the rest of her life. The last thing Zora needed was ammunition, not after the lifetime they'd lived together fueling her with enough to make fodder of for eternity.

"Hey, you never finished telling me your idea about algae incentives."

"Well, I don't know if it's an idea. Just a thought."

"Babe, can you just say it without downplaying it? We have an agenda as soon as the water warms up."

He laughed. "Okay, good point. Right. It's a brilliant idea that I had entirely because you dragged me into working on the Surfside Swell Expo."

"Pretty sure you need to yell at your siblings for that one."

"Okay, regardless. You know the Surfside Swell website?"

She nodded.

"Well, you were talking about your database of the micro-algae and how you're trying to get that job working on ecosystems and ocean based communities, right? So the Surfside site has this map of the town, and then these interactive overlays for various things. Woman and BIPOC owned businesses, places that've signed the fair wage pledge. Unionized shops. I don't know how all the overlay stuff works, but you know Quinn?"

"Yeah?"

"They're the one who designed the site, so they could tell you all the technical stuff, but. You know also how I have my nontraditional way of understanding data? So when you told me about your roadmap for the carbon dioxide removal pathways, I thought you could do something like that, and, like, map the existing resources onto the network, and that way show where everything intersects and where there are different kinds of distinct needs? So that's it. Is it something that would be useful to you? I'm not trying to—I'm sure what you've already got for your capstone is amazing. Everything you told me is amazing to me. I was trying to think of a way that it would make more sense to me and—"

She pulled him in for a kiss and at that moment probably wouldn't have noticed, much less cared, if anybody had sauntered in and caught them. "Stop downplaying it. I love it and I'm definitely implementing it. Thanks."

"It's only that the way you explained it was really straightforward? And I'm not a straightforward person, generally speaking. Like, it wasn't until Quinn started doing the overlays on the Surfside Swell site that I noticed where there were kind of distinct areas of inclusion and exclusion. Abraham was like, 'Well, duh, those spots are all where chain stores have encroached, or else they're the higher socioeconomic areas where everything is zoned residential.' But that genuinely never occurred to me until I saw it on the map."

She kept nudging him towards the shower. And he kept rambling. Even once she'd checked the water temp and complimented the mural on the shower walls, he just switched to talking about laying the tiles.

"You're cute, but hush now. I've been lured into getting naked with my man in a public—semi-public, but as close as'll ever happen—so I'm going to make the most of it, if you don't mind."

He finally went still and hushed. Then said, all husky and intent with an undercurrent of absolute pleasure, "Your man?"

She wrapped her arms over his shoulders and let him take the bulk of the shower spray. "Kissing you on the pier and spending the night and putting up with our friends teasing? That's more than casual for me, Austin. Even before you took my work seriously and came up with a way I can graphically showcase my conclusions."

Next thing she knew, her back was to that pretty tile and he was kneeling between her legs and she sure as hell hoped the doors stayed locked and the floors were soundproofed because there was semi-public and there was public, and she had noises to make that no one but she and Austin needed to hear.

Chapter Twenty

He'd been watching her on the waves all morning. Austin wasn't clear exactly how he could pick Leyla out of dark line of surfers the second she popped up on Rainbow and smoothed into a barrel, but sometimes his brain did stuff like that. Kept background track of how many bodies were in the lineup and the pace of the waves. When it was about time for her to break in, his subconscious prompted him to be looking out the window and watch as it became clear that it was indeed Leyla carving her way towards shore, only to pull up in the whitewater and paddle back to the lineup.

It made his shift fly by, tracking her movements, storing up comments to share later about the others in her paddle out, who she wouldn't see when sitting behind the swells. The guy who kept dropping in—his background thoughts realized just then that was another marker of when he could expect to see Leyla, since intrusive assholes pulled their shit on women in a lineup way more than on men. The guy who got caught inside so long it seemed like he'd be duck-diving forever. The pure beauty of Noah standing goofy foot on the crest of a three-foot swell.

Okay, he also recognized Noah in the group of same-same neoprene black shapes. Probably because his cousin was wearing that reflective hood of his that gave him a halo he hadn't earned.

Also, because Noah was the one to cut back in the pocket and hold, waiting on Leyla to ride the foam to shore with him. They crossed to Pier Three together, chatting every moment. He had their drinks ready to go by the time they'd rinsed and stashed their boards and pulled flip-flops and shirts out of the storage lockers.

"What's this?"

"Hazelnut latte." He acted like he didn't get the point of her question. She rotated the reusable steel mug he'd etched her name into.

"It's so pretty. And mine all mine. I love it."

He shrugged to continue his feigned nonchalance. "I had some new tools to etch my initials in. Thought I could do this for you at the same time. "

"Where's mine?" Noah asked.

Austin handed him a tray with a flat white and a croissant and all his hopes that his cousin would take the hint and leave them be.

"Noah isn't as many letters as Leyla. It's only one more letter than your initials. Hell, half of your initials are in my name, Austin Octavio Wells. Seems like making me a personalized mug wouldn't be much of a problem."

"And yet."

Noah ignored his flat tone. "That's what I'm saying. You know, when you were a little kid, you'd go out of your way to hero-worship me. Infuriated your brother, so I encouraged it, but you came up with the idolatry all on your own. Whatever happened to that? Back then you'd have made me a mug without me having to point out how neglected I feel."

"Noah. If I swear to etch your name on a reusable mug,

will you give me and Leyla five minutes alone? I have inter-views for a new hire all morning and I don't want prospective employees' first impressions of the place to be me throttling any of my relatives."

He snickered. "But it's fine for them to see you making out with a customer, I guess? Seems like you'd wait until orien-tation to show them how much fraternization they can get away with."

Austin reached to the under-counter fridge and snagged a beet juice. "Now will you go away?"

"Bribe accepted." Noah plucked it from him, then kissed Leyla's cheek. "You're worth more than a coffee and a pastry, and don't you ever forget it."

"Fraternization?"

He huffed. "I don't have rules about that. Unless a customer feels unsafe, of course. There's a reporting portal on the app so they can make complaints. And the box by the door."

"What if the customer is the one making your staff feel unsafe?"

His shrug was like, duh, it's self-evident. "Banned."

She tipped her head to a two-top. "Got time to sit before your interviews start?"

"Come on back to the office, so I can run over a couple things."

"And so no one sees us kissing?" She masked her smile behind a sip of the latte in her shiny new personalized multi-use mug.

She'd probably glimpsed the office before, going through the back door or to the restroom, but never been inside. It was snug, between the shelves of baked goods and coffee supplies, some kind of industrial fridge, a filing cabinet and desk, and the two of them. Austin solved the space problem by pulling her into his lap while he sat on the one chair.

"You're gonna get soaked."

"Hmm. That's true. Want me to help you take this the rest of the way off?"

Next time, she was packing a sundress instead of just a t-shirt, and never mind how that meant traipsing, uncaffeinated, back to her car to stash her wetsuit while she loitered inside with Austin. Being around him just plain made her want bare legs.

"What time is your interview? Did someone give notice, or what?"

"Yeah, no. Cleo's fam is moving so if she kept her schedule it would take two busses to get here now. She wants to cut back hours to be when she can get the express." He gestured back to a wall covered in sticky notes. His bedroom had the same sort of setup. "I've got to fill the gaps."

"You know there's this invention called a spreadsheet."

"Ha. Cute. I told you about how I process info my own unique and special way. This is it."

"Oh!" She bounced a bit and slung her arm across his shoulder. "Guess what? Quinn's meeting me back here in a bit. They're open to me hiring them to create the overlays for my capstone."

He kissed her soundly, but swiftly, and asked, "So that's really going to work for you?"

"Yes, Sir Doubts-a-lot."

Maybe her tone was a little impatient. Not because she didn't get why he had his issues being confident in his ideas, but because she wanted to get back to the kissing. He'd entirely stopped letting his hand creep up towards her bikini top to talk, and she was buoyant from a morning communing with the ocean, and those two things were not compatible.

Nature wanted her keep riding a high. Austin wanted her to talk.

"Sorry."

"No. That's me being snippy. I'm sorry. Plus, I need to get cleaned up—can I change upstairs so I don't have to wriggle into clothes in my car? And you need to do whatever work it is you claimed was a priority when you lured me back here."

He flip-switched to sexy intent again. "The work I want to do requires you taking off your wetsuit."

"How long do you have, seriously? Because I already claimed dibs on the upstairs bathroom again."

He checked one of the papers taped to the wall. "Yes, you can have the bathroom, but the Santos's are up in one of the studios, editing. And my soundproofing is good, but maybe not 'Leyla coming for the third time' good."

"Third time?" She wriggled. It wasn't easy to grind with four millimeters of neoprene between her clit and Austin's thigh, but she let herself rock a few times against him, just for the fun memories to enjoy later.

They made do with making out and a bunch more kissing before either had to get on with the non-sexy parts of their lives. As they left the office, Austin said, "Hang on," and took one of the many sticky notes off the wall, handing it to her.

"Diana and Issac?" She looked to him, because a scrawled couple of names followed by a row of interconnected hearts and a leaping fish didn't translate to what he'd probably call her mainstream way of synthesizing information.

"The Santos siblings. You'll probably run into them upstairs. They do a bunch with the Norbay Podcast Network, and I was telling them about your algae. I'm sure I messed up the specifics, but the point it, they want to see if you'll be interviewed on one of their shows. Or one of the shows they edit? I think their own pod is just about fishing. Anyhow, if you don't see them in the studios, I'll share your contact with them and they can ask you directly. If it's okay. I told them since it's the last term of your MS, you might be too busy even if you're interested, and they said they totally get that. So it's no pressure."

Did Austin even realize what a connector he always was? She'd noticed it before, how whenever he got to talking with someone—and he was always talking to so many someones—he mentioned a third or fourth or fifth party they should meet, to the benefit of everyone. Or everyone who wasn't him, since he didn't seek to advance himself, far as she could tell.

Just one more way he was the opposite of Chad, who didn't know how to live without looking out for his own interests first.

Maybe that was a pitfall of academia, because Chad was hardly the only operator in her cohort. He was just the one who irritated her the most. And not entirely because what he wanted was too close to what she wanted for herself.

"I'll introduce myself. Is the fish because that's their primary interest?"

He curled himself around her to examine the message he'd given her, then clunked his head to her shoulder. "If I admit to that, do I have to say what the hearts are for, too?"

She kissed his temple. "I think I figured that part out already."

He growled, but didn't contradict whatever assumptions she was allowing herself to make.

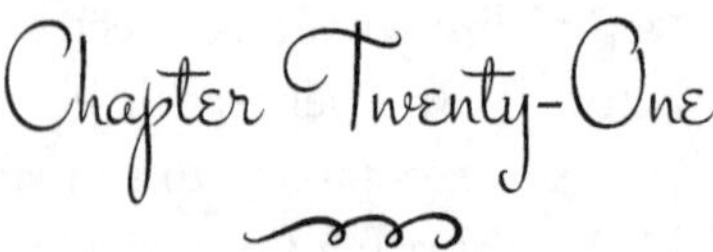

Chapter Twenty-One

"I swear we had these lengthy conversations about you and Callie moving in together. We toured places while she was in New Hampshire. You signed a lease and packed up your shit. Any of this ring a bell?" Austin flopped on their couch next to Abe, who'd shown up in the middle of the night—well, middle of the night for Austin, so ten p.m. or something— and disappeared straight into his bedroom without a word.

When morning came, he found his brother's ass planted in the divots he'd worn into the couch long ago. He didn't look at all like he'd be leaving soon. "Trouble in paradise?"

The look is Abraham gave him. *Ha.* His ego was super affronted by the idea that he would allow anything approaching trouble to interfere with his and Callie's love story. Austin pulled out the game controllers, passing the adaptive one to Abe, who'd left his prosthetic behind when he crashed the apartment. They started in on their current favorite co-op, collecting lives and teaming up to defeat levels.

The peace of their electronic combat was shattered when the door opened and their parents walked in. Austin grabbed his stuffed elephant, a relic of his youth he'd hung on to for sentimental reasons but which, it turned out, was also handy to have around when he didn't particularly want his parents to know he wore boxer briefs printed with marijuana leaves.

Abe snickered. "By the way, Mom and Dad are coming down to take us to breakfast."

Austin had his avatar turn and push Abe's off a cliff. Abraham responded with a one arm salute, but he was also so busy snarfling to himself like he was some kind of pranking genius that there wasn't a lot of heat to it.

"Abraham Augustus Wells." Their mom's voice held her usual utter reverence for her firstborn underneath any kind of scolding or commentary she had for him. "You weren't going to tell your brother we were coming?"

Abe shrugged. "I got distracted."

Dad walked up and put hands on both their shoulders, leaning between them to distribute kisses. "We'll go look at that bathroom repair you've been doing while you get some clothes on, yeah?"

"Sure thing, Dad."

He managed to stop his brother from wrestling his elephant away until their folks were out of sight. Then Abe pulled on the trunk with enough force he worried it'd rip if he didn't let go. "You fucking ass."

Abe just laughed harder. Austin suspected he'd be receiving yet another couple pairs of novelty boxer shorts his next birthday. He guessed it was the only thing his brother could ever think of to buy him. He was just glad he hadn't slipped on the ones with the sexy bunnies or the ones with the photorealistic wolf snout covering his junk.

Once they were all presentable, they opted for The Tides Cafe. His dad spent the ride naming every favorite thing of his in Austin's remodel of the bathroom. The work had been necessary thanks to an overflowing toilet in the apartment upstairs collapsing his ceiling. He'd grabbed the excuse to upgrade his countertop and fixtures, repaint the whole room, and install new mirrors, including a fog-free one for shaving. He especially liked his new backsplash tile, a silver and lavender fish scale pattern that shimmered like a mermaid in the dawn mist under his new frosted glass light fittings. He'd debated between those or the ones like aging driftwood, but when he brought the samples of each home to experiment, the driftwood ones grayed to blahness against his sage paint.

Something in his dad's expression, once they all agreed he'd made great choices, urged him to order both the waffles and the migas. "Hold the cilantro. Thanks. And Dad, what's going on?"

Not that the family didn't go out for breakfast periodically. But usually they were spontaneous, or he was in on the plans from the beginning.

"Also, is Licie coming or what?" They'd asked for a table for four, but he might as well check.

"Well, no, we didn't need to talk to her, sweetie," Mom said. "The reason we asked Abraham to tell you about breakfast today—"

Divine intervention came in the form of their server with coffee, which he knocked back not even caring that he hadn't yet persuaded Tides' owners to go in on his ethically sourced beans collective. He needed the caffeine to redirect the jackrabbit in his stomach. Hearing that Mom had recruited Abraham specifically to drag him to brunch this morning? Now his brother's sleeping at the apartment made sense. He was tasked with stopping Austin from being a flight risk, even though nobody bothered to alert him there was something he'd want to fly from.

Abraham passed over his fresh squeezed orange juice, like that was some sort of compensation or apology. He passed it right back, because whatever his brother thought he needed amends for, he was gonna make up his own mind to grant or withhold them.

Abe shrugged and chugged his juice, which Mom marked with a chiding but still loving "Abraham."

Dad interrupted to ask stuff about Callie. Dad was a huge fan of Callie, and not just for her artistic skill and success. To him, she was a paragon of loving support, first in the years that she and Alicia had been friends and roommates, and now on top of that because she had worked with Abraham until they figured out a way to meld their lives in a committed partnership.

Reinforcing her belief that Austin was sorely lacking because he didn't have a partner who took care of him, Mom said, "I wish that all my babies could have the mutual support that you and Callie have. Or that Alicia and Mateo do."

"So, me," Austin said, and even the divine interruption of entrees didn't scrape anything caustic off his words. "You're talking just about me. You wish someone would come along and take care of me. It doesn't matter what I do or how I succeed. You've never thought I'm competent to stand on my own, and now that Abraham doesn't live with me anymore you're worried I'm gonna, what? Burn down the place? Refuse to help our tenants? Fall into a coma and not be discovered until I've missed a dozen shifts at the cafe?"

"Oh, Austin." It wasn't fondness underneath Mom's words. "We would discover you much sooner than that."

"Besides, I understand you're seeing someone now." Dad gave him a smile full of relieved happiness.

"Are you? Oh, that's lovely news. Do we know her? Is it a her? It's okay if it's not."

Abraham laughed, which might have been annoying but Austin would have, too, if the tone of the conversation wasn't setting his alarms off. He'd been obviously and vocally interested in women since he was in elementary school.

"It's a woman. She's called Leyla and we know from the cafe," Abraham told them. "She's a getting her doctorate in climate change at the university."

"Master's in Coastal Science and Policy," he corrected, too late realizing that Abe had set him up by deliberately mislabeling her academic career.

He focused on adding just the right combination of Cholula and creamy jalapeño salsa to his eggs while his family exclaimed and rejoiced and tossed in just enough pointed commentary to remind him of their doubt Leyla was in his league: "Oh, if this is her final year of the Masters, that's got to take so much of her time." "And she went into the MS straight after her Bachelor's? She must have known since high school what she wanted to do with her life." "Well, of course if she's going to get a doctorate next—do you know if she's getting a doctorate?" And, after ignoring his assurances that she was not: "She could end up anywhere in the world doing high level research with a doctorate in that field. It's thrilling that she's taking on this work. I'd love to know how she got started."

He swallowed down each little barb with a square of waffles drenched in maple syrup. The sweetness didn't do much to help his emotions stay down.

They were in danger of finishing this meal without his folks revealing why they'd gone to such lengths to set it up, so he interrupted their odes to a woman they'd never met to say, "We've only had one date, but I will introduce you if it ever goes anywhere. Can you tell me what's going on that made you have Abraham hold me captive today?"

Mom took a deep breath, her expression carefully pleasant. "For a while now we've been collecting bids from different management companies to take over the apartments."

Austin dropped his fork to the plate and pushed it away. "Excuse me?" He looked at Abraham, who shook his head. Good thing too, because if his brother knew about this, and that this was the reason for the ambush, there'd be more than hell to pay.

"We're getting older, Austin," Dad said. "We're wanting to have adventures."

"You're not even sixty yet."

"Yes, I am."

"You are?"

"Remember last spring, we rented out the party room at the Korean barbecue place?"

Austin grumbled. But yeah, he did actually remember that. It made sense it would have been for some milestone thing like his dad's sixtieth. He nodded in apologetic acceptance. "But what do you mean by you've been planning this a while?"

"Pretty much since Granny died," Mom said. "By then, with you three out of school and ..." She trailed off rather than add something about how Austin had dropped out of college after all of his years of stops and starts and changing majors. She was obviously trying to be gentle with him, so she didn't say it explicitly.

Of course, she didn't need to speak aloud for Austin to understand what she was thinking.

She shrugged. "With that all done and us not needing to live in town for your granny anymore, we figured it was time to turn it over to someone else."

He shot a look at Dad, who met his eyes for only a second before looking away. It was all Austin needed to prove his dad remembered the times they'd talked about him taking over not just the superintendent job, but also as building manager one day. Not that Austin had ever brought it back up himself. He hadn't figured his dad was ready to stop working just yet, which shows what he knew.

Years this had been going on behind his back. Years of him thinking it was a done deal, that once Pier Three was established and they'd move past the demands of the recession, he would have freed up his time to take on the management role. Years of thinking his parents would retire, leaving him as de facto landlord, with Abraham on his team doing the books. But: no. They'd been talking to management companies and never once said, "Austin, if you want to run this building one day you'll need to get your degree," or "Austin, we've changed our minds and don't want your unworthy mitts anywhere near the resource we've spent our lives building."

Abraham flagged down someone to refill their coffees. Not that he wanted to drag this whole conversation out any longer, but he appreciated having the warm drink to stabilize him a bit while they got through it.

"In the end, we didn't sign with them," Mom said.

He flashed her a glance to see if this was some sort of torturous, roundabout way of saying they'd changed their minds about him.

It wasn't.

"The people who own Cypress Villas? They heard we were interviewing and reached out with an offer to buy instead. It ..." She grimaced across at him. Rested her hand for a moment on Abraham's arm.

"It's good," Dad said. "We're taking it. But, Austin, we made sure they would keep you on as super. We're writing it into the contract. They have to give you at least a year in the job, or two month's notice if there's going to be a change. We don't want you to be tossed out without time to deal with it, obviously. Besides, they're lucky to have you. Everyone loves you and appreciates the work you do."

He snorted. It didn't release any of the pressure like copper coils round his rib cage. "You can tell 'everyone' thanks, but no thanks. I'm not an albatross tied round the building you have to apologize for in your negotiations. Unless you mean to say I've kept my job—my home—out of pity all these years? That it was the only thing you two could think up to keep me from drifting out to sea? If these Cypress Villas people think I'm as useless as you do, that's fine. They can fire me anytime. Cause like I said before, I'm totally capable of taking care of myself."

It was a good exit line, and he wasn't in the mood to brawl, or to bawl, in public. So he dropped a tip on the table and walked out.

Chapter Twenty-Two

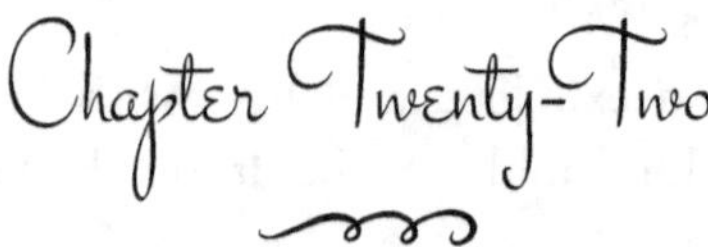

"How's the romance going? Are you in love yet?"

"We've had exactly one date," Leyla said. Maybe she sounded huffy, but not because she and Austin hadn't scheduled another sleepover yet. She knew they would get to it. She just didn't like being the busy one whose life kept her sleeping alone too much. Case in point: she had to multitask drafting emails to her capstone Readers while talking to her sister. Case further in point: her sister was the one who had to call her for an update for once, since she was so slammed, she was letting her regular check-ins slide.

"Exactly one date that ended exactly in his bed." Zora sang the last few words. She thought she was so funny.

"Well, it was a good date. It was still just the once."

"So you haven't seen him since?"

"I mean ..."

Zora cackled at her, which was downright exasperating. Fair, but exasperating.

"We've run across each other a time or two," she admitted.

"Are those two times when you've gone deliberately to his cafe and sat there until he kissed you senseless?"

"Be quiet." Leyla sat back and rubbed her too-much-screen-time eyes. "Tell me something about you, or home. The only news you've shared lately is that Lance's got a new car."

"It's a nice car. Hybrid SUV."

"And I'm happy for him, but I'm guessing the entire city of Phoenix didn't shut down to observe his test drive. What else is going on?"

Zora made the kind of throat clearing that presaged her avoiding a topic.

She pounced. "Okay, something is going on. What is it? Do I worry?"

"You know I wouldn't do that to you."

"You'd better not."

"Did you just try to threaten me, baby sister?" Zora asked. "And relax. It's just more of the usual nonsense."

She paused her clicking around and trying to get her work organized. "What's that mean?"

Zora clucked. "Nothing. You know we had that barbecue for Mom and Dad's anniversary?"

"Of course." She'd FaceTimed Mom's phone, which got passed around the party from person to person until the battery died.

"Right. So, Dad's telling his sibs how we're all coming up for your graduation, right? And then Granmama bops over to expostulate to them about how the percentage gap of Black people with advanced degrees is narrowing thanks to people like you, and how it's especially cool that your degree is in a field where we're still underrepresented. Which ..."

"Ugh."

"Right?"

None of what Mom's mama had said was a lie. And none of it was going to endear her one whit to her dad's side of the family. "Any chance someone came along and said yes, Granmama, that's why we're focused on celebrating Leyla instead of casting aspersions on everyone else in the world?"

"Cute. No. Not so as I heard."

"And tell me why am I just now finding out about this? That party was almost two weeks ago."

"My sweet Lance forgot to tell me." Leyla could tell from her mock-sigh and sweet tone that Lance was in the room with her. Sure enough, she heard his apology in the background.

"Too caught up in car shopping, I gather. Makes sense. But Dad should have mentioned it. We were just talking the other day."

"Oh, did you tell him about Austin? Maybe he was too shook by the thought of his baby having sexual relations to remember holding his sister back from expressing her every thought to his mother-in-law."

"Ew. 'Sexual relations?' Stop. Or do you want me to tell him about why you and Lance had to get a new mattress pad?"

Zora screamed and relayed the threat to Lance, who added his shriek of laughter to the mix. Served them right for letting her know about that whole situation in the first place.

ALICIA: You know our folks don't mean it, right?

ABRAHAM: of course he knows it

ALICIA: I mean, of course he does

ALICIA: I'm saying for the record though since I didn't get an invite to brunch like the rest of you

ALICIA: not that I'm complaining

ABRAHAM: clearly not

ABRAHAM: and you didn't miss much not being there

ALICIA: I'll never know, will I?

ALICIA: I might have really enjoyed listening to Dad pretend none of this impacts anyone else

ALICIA: Like, suddenly they don't want to stick in town just to be near the rest of the family? To us? Are they moving out of the building? Are they buying a house with spare bedrooms for when the grandkids sleep over? Are they renting an RV and driving around the country forever?

ABRAHAM: grandkids?

AUSTIN: Grandkids??!

ALICIA: HA, got you to respond

ABRAHAM: I don't think they meant an RV when they said adventures

ALICIA: See, I wouldn't know, since I wasn't invited to brunch. And I'd have asked, unlike you two

AUSTIN: was a little busy being interrogated and kicked out of my home so sorry I didn't ask the right follow up questions

ABRAHAM: they did not kick you out

AUSTIN: don't be literal at me. Especially when we all know they'd never be doing this if you still lived here. Not when Mom could wander down for your company anytime she missed you too much

ABRAHAM: hey

ALICIA: huh. yeah. Suspicious timing, no matter what they claimed about Cypress Villas

AUSTIN: I'm saying

ABRAHAM: after you left Dad asked if you smoke a lot of pot

ALICIA: ??????????

ABRAHAM: he was only wearing boxers when they came to drive us to the accursed brunch

ALICIA: I repeat ???? Does it mean you're high if you aren't dressed in the morning?

AUSTIN: omg I hate you both

ABRAHAM: [*link: men's novelty boxer briefs*]

ALICIA: ew ew ew stop

ALICIA: ew

ALICIA: I hate you both

ABRAHAM: love you, don't forget monthly meeting tomorrow

AUSTIN: How do your roommates feel about guys stopping by to cook for everyone and then spending the night

AUSTIN: with just you, I mean. Not spending the night with them

AUSTIN: or not spending the night with you, if you don't have time. But I finished training Elmer early. And (pitiful excuse alert) you said we need to go over the Expo stuff

AUSTIN: or

AUSTIN: if I'm being annoying, I can just email you the Expo updates, and I will definitely not expire from not kissing you in the meanwhile.

AUSTIN: I will definitely live to kiss you another day. It's worth living for

AUSTIN: I'm doing my homework now so don't worry I will stop sending giant text chains

AUSTIN: last one, I swear: you're very pretty and I like you very much

LEYLA: new phone who dis?

AUSTIN: gah I had my notifications turned all the way up and just fell off the sofa

LEYLA: You doing your homework or are you gaming?

AUSTIN: ... is both an option?

LEYLA: Do you still have time to hang out, or is that homework a problem?

AUSTIN: my only problem is not being near you

LEYLA: I warned you about the cheese, sir

AUSTIN: answer the question!

LEYLA: excuse me while I scroll a mile back to find your original question, might take a minute

AUSTIN: me, food, bed?

LEYLA: yes, no, no.

LEYLA: don't fall off the sofa again

AUSTIN: I won't - I'm busy weeping into the cushions

LEYLA: yes, I have time to see you

LEYLA: no, no one minds if you cook for us

LEYLA: no, my roommates aren't up for sleepovers - we have a pact to keep them to Saturday nights if any of us are swamped (which two of us are)

AUSTIN: whew. okay. I should come by with food, then, at least?

LEYLA: Or

AUSTIN: or?

LEYLA: Or you could turn off the very loud video game and answer your door.

Chapter Twenty-Three

"You're here."

He was all energy and attention everywhere while he swept through the apartment shoving things into place like she thought he lived a monastic life. But also, all of his attention was on her, talking and touches in passing and scraping his hair into place and asking what she wanted for dinner.

In other words, he was very much himself. And that was exactly what she was in the mood for. When it had happened, she couldn't say precisely. But all the teasing and all the flirting and all the coffee and the texting and the sitting in Pier Three doing her own thing while he did his own thing. And the sex, which lived up not just to his promises but also to any kind of standard she'd ever imagined. All that. Every bit of it.

It meant that she was mush for Austin.

When he started to clear the dining table of his schoolwork, she stopped him. "I brought my laptop. In case you were going to accuse me of showing up just to get laid."

"Ha. Please show up to get laid anytime you like." He wrapped them together and two-stepped them through the room. "Matter of fact, give me three minutes and I'll run out to my shop and cut you a set of keys. Midnight, five a.m., high noon. I'm at your disposal."

She pulled him to land over her on the couch. "If you have three minutes to spare, Dawn Patrol, I have better ideas."

"Yeah?" His hips slid in a half-circle across hers. "Only three minutes? I like a challenge. Let's do it."

Laughing together with him had this way of more than doubling her pleasure. It was an exponential experience.

Maybe the same phenomenon happened when they were kissing. It wasn't just his nips and lips and licks, plus her tongue and hums. It was all of it, mixing and morphing into something so much greater than the sum of their parts.

And that was one explanation for how she had her first orgasm three minutes after their first kiss of the night.

Another reason had to do with how quickly Austin rucked up her skirt and kissed his way from her knees to her thighs while he palmed her ass cheeks and told her with growling half-syllables that he was going to devour her pussy then finger her to another peak then tease her clit just enough for it to know he was only giving it a temporary break while he tasted every slope of her stomach and breasts.

And how he went on to do everything he promised.

So that explained the next couple of orgasms. The fourth, she didn't know how to define or categorize. Some part of her must have learned to operate the way Austin did, with leaps onto tracks she'd never have imagined. How else could she understand coming just from dirty talk, and watching him rip his clothes off, and the burst of glee when she saw his boxers were covered with knights jousting with dildos?

Sure, she was thumbing her throbbing clit at the time, but there was so much more to it.

She lunged forward to stop him from removing the ridiculous things. "What in the holy hell happened to make you buy these?"

"I didn't."

"Okay, but explain more please?" Her fingers danced over all the cartoon warriors.

"My brother buys all these joke boxers for me. He knows I hate it."

She nibbled at one of the neon pink dildos. It was in a particularly sweet and musky spot, and his cock jerked. "Then why do you wear them?"

"I never used to, not much. If I ran out of my own I'd raid his dresser. Then he moved out, and I came to find out he packed up all of his own and also all my normal pairs. Nothing left but a whole drawer full of this shit." He pinched at the hem and shrugged.

Leyla traced a pair of combatants running at each other along his waistline. "Wait. The other day, weren't those plain?"

"I'm going shopping tomorrow."

"When there's a whole drawer like this for me to explore? Rude." She jacked him once then fixed him with an expectant stare. "What about the other day?"

He sighed. "One side of the ass has a shark, and the other side a speech bubble saying 'bite me.' Can we drop it now?"

She helped him drop the knights to the floor. And then she dropped to her knees.

Good hell and heaven and every kind of pleasure spot in between.

Leyla, kneeling in front of him.

Leyla, warm hands traveling up his thighs.

Actual, for real, Leyla Robinson tracing her superb lips with her tantalizing tongue, taking in his erection.

A shudder flowed through him, which he hoped she didn't see, not that she ever seemed to mind the ways he bounced and vibrated three-quarters of the time he was awake.

That was the other thing. It wasn't just that it was Leyla Robinson, most perfect beauty brainy strong and soft and perfect woman, who had him in hand.

This was Leyla, a friend who teased him about his weaknesses and made him stronger.

This was Leyla, a companion who listened to his fears and trusted he would overcome them.

This was Leyla, a lover who kindled his inner fire and met him in the flames.

All those months and years of crushing on her from not-so-much-distance, he didn't really know her. Didn't know how it would be when it was him and her. He'd only had guesses.

Fantasies.

Leyla, the real Leyla and not the one he made up to torment his lonely soul, outmatched anything he'd imagined.

And that was before she darted her tongue across his slit and asked if he wanted to come down her throat.

"Oh fuck."

"Not an answer."

"Are you comfortable there? You need a cushion?" She was glorious, dress rumpled, glasses perched in her hair, and eyes darting between his face and his aching, leaking, extremely interested cock.

"Austin. I'm comfy as can be, as long as you don't wait another hour to answer my question."

Damn bless his soul, but he was lucky. "Suck. Don't make me come."

That earned him another squeeze to his base. "What I do is up to me. What you don't do—that's your job. Stop yourself if you can."

And she didn't give him a second to reply. Not that he had

words. Words and he had problems connecting when Leyla was near, this wasn't news to him. He was learning that the problem got worse, the less they were wearing.

And he wasn't wearing anything. Not even ridiculous boxer briefs.

He wanted to brace himself, to hold her head. But her glasses were perched in her hair. So he settled one hand on the side of her neck, and the other—the other flailed. He couldn't help it. Leyla's tongue did clever and wild things around his shaft as she hollowed her cheeks around him. He unraveled and came back together in wholly new and exciting ways, just because she dug her fingers real close to the crack of his ass and lifted her chin just enough to destabilize whatever core had been holding him together.

His other hand fell to her shoulder, and it was maybe the only thing keeping him upright as she increased her tempo and he fought to keep his eyes open. To memorize the sight of Leyla's lips curving around his cock. And the way she tilted an eye up at him, her look full of glint and fire and fun.

She hummed and his knees buckled a little. "Devil." Because it was hard. It was maybe impossible. The heat and wet and motion and noise and Leyla of it all.

His spine couldn't withstand it. His balls ached and those fucking knights could win any tournament lancing with his steel cock. And she wasn't pulling off, no matter how he thrust and thrust into the bliss of her mouth, and every time he said her name she did something pulse-ramping with her tongue.

He …

She …

He groaned. The sound started in his toes and ripped up through his entire body, and it was the force he needed to release her and urge her to her feet.

"Austin."

He kissed her swollen lips, hard. Not as hard as his cock was hard, because no one needed to kiss a statue, but plaster-her-to-his-mouth hard. Hitching her legs around his waist, which was another agony of sensation—silky damp underwear sliding and rubbing his erection, skirt hem fluttering too light and too flirty against his thighs—he hustled them to his bed.

"I'm going to fuck you now." He dropped her to the mattress and helped her strip. Tossed all her clothes away like they offended him, which at the moment they did. Reached for a condom and when she moved like she was going to help him with it, narrowed his eyes. "Touch me again now and I'll come before I get this on."

"You say that like I'd mind."

He guided her hand between her own legs. "Spread yourself for me, Leyla. Damn. Look at that, yes. Your lips all open and wet and welcoming. Beautiful. Wait, here." He flipped open the lube and squeezed some onto her fingers, then some on the condom.

"Going to make a mess of your sheets, huh?"

"I have spares. Rub yourself. Get your pretty clit all thrumming and enticed. Fuck. Leyla, yes. That's it. See how your nipples went hard when you did that? I'm going to remember that for later, that's a promise. Will you keep rubbing when I'm in you? Cause I'm—"

He couldn't finish the sentence. She took his entire length in one slick slide, and it was all he could do to not drive himself to completion in two hard greedy thrusts. He sent his hips to rocking against hers, keeping it shallow, but every motion, any motion, he found her fingers at work. His base nudged and pressed and tilted, and it all left her panting. Her body was squeezing his shaft and he drew back to give her room to work her clit, which meant he could fully see her face —the way she was looking at him, the way she half-laughed and caught her tongue with her teeth and raised her brows like she had things to say if only he could be listening to their bodies.

So he did. He listened to the way she pulsed when he sheathed his full length in her. The way she upped the tempo of her circling fingers when he pulled out. The way she gripped his upper arm, and the way his breath sped up, and the way their slick skin slap slap slapped together as he thrust. The way she tipped her pelvis while he thrust again, and again, and again again again until she cried out his name and dragged him down to kiss him with ferocious intent. Until he thrust again, hard, hardest yet, lost in her heat and in their motion.

Until he came, deep and long, and full, and complete in her arms.

Chapter Twenty-Four

His body curled around hers so close she felt his heartbeat. Or maybe it was hers pounding everywhere like the thrill-seeker he seemed to think she was. It felt safe, though, beating however madcap it wanted pressed up against Austin's warmth. They slid into a doze, messy sheets and all. Next thing she knew, he was nudging her awake, offering her a bottle of water and a warm t-shirt.

"Fresh from the dryer. Dinner's ready when you are."

Leyla downed the water and stretched. She'd fallen into a nap, which never happened. She wasn't a nap person.

She wasn't so many things, if she'd told the story of herself a couple months back. Not a napper, or a community organizer, or an expert interviewee on podcasts, or someone who veered anywhere off the rails of the life she'd mapped for herself years ago.

Life near Austin was life without a spreadsheet. And maybe she liked it?

"Where's my clothes?"

"Dress is hanging from the shower rail. I put your underthings in the machine for a quick wash."

When she stood, she flashed him a look. She wasn't one of those waifs—or he wasn't one of those giants—where wearing her man's shirt covered her legs halfway down to her knees. He straightened with the bedsheets in a bundle. "Don't guess I can persuade you to walk around my apartment like that?"

"Nope. Where's this collection of underpants humor of yours?" She didn't wait for him to answer, just pulled open his top dresser drawer, selected a pair of socks, and opened the next drawer over. "Oh sweet lord. You weren't kidding."

He only had a few pairs of boxers, each sillier than the last. Roosters and busty rabbits and dancing bananas and ones saying 'pull down in case of emergency' across the front. "Where are the 'bite me' ones?"

"In the basket. I just took them from dryer."

She picked the ones with hot dog buns and followed him from the room like it was the end of the conversation. As if. She hadn't missed the way he'd backed to the door and held the sheets low to hide whatever he'd pulled on during her nap.

"You want me to wash your dress, too? I didn't see if you brought spare clothes."

Her messenger bag had everything she'd need to spend the night, but instead of elucidating him, she crowded in as he stood in front of his stacked washer/dryer. He reached up and pulled out a mesh bag with her bra and undies and tossed it in the dryer. "Is that okay, or do you not tumble dry your delicates? I can hang them instead. Also, I hope you like spinach. There's a lot in this soup I made. The bread'll be out of the oven in two minutes. It's a peasant loaf, just baked from frozen but I like it."

She kept silent, because it was hilarious how he started babbling when he was avoiding something like bending down to pick up the sheets he needed to heft into the wash.

Finally he turned. "Fine. You're obviously not going to let it go. Look your fill." He spread his arms wide, which caused his shirt to ride up so she could behold the full glory of what encased his crotch and ass.

"Is that ... Rainbow Sparkle? Wait, no. Sparklefly? Is she called Sparklefly?" Good thing there was a dining chair right there, 'cause she couldn't stay upright for all the laughter.

"Twilight Sparkle, thanks very much." He brushed a hand over the unicorn pony prancing over the front of his baby blue shorts. "This one's Pinky Pie, and Fluttershy's on the back."

She uncovered her mouth long enough to make a 'spin' gesture. It was all too perfect, and she was absolutely going to high-five Abraham next time she saw him.

"Rainbow Dash!" She totally recognized the one on his left ass cheek.

"Yeah, yeah, Rainbow Dash. If you start singing a theme song, I'm going to be the one pounding on my neighbor's door for a rescue."

"Don't worry, my stomach's too doubled over with laughter for me to take the breath I'd need to sing."

Austin shoved the sheets into the washer. "Am I adding your dress in here or no?"

"I used to wonder what friendship could be."

He stalked to her, which was a trick given there were only a few feet separating them, and stood straddling her thighs. "Is that a no?"

Look at him, trying to keep her on topic. What reversed roles they were playing. She decided to go with the flow and kiss her way up his happy trail to his navel and nuzzle into his abdomen.

"God, Leyla. You're too much." He held her head to his torso, running a finger across the part in her scalp and down her nape and making her shiver into his warmth. They stayed like that, balanced in restful energy like the lull between swells, until a timer beeped.

He bent to kiss her. "That's the bread. Sit tight, I'll get dinner."

Instead of following his suggestion, she retrieved her dress from the bathroom and figured out how to operate his washing machine. Then while he ladled up bowls of soup and sliced and buttered the bread, she shifted the books and papers into smaller piles on the table so they'd have room to spread out.

She didn't mean to stop mid-organizing and read his assignment.

"Do you want help with this?"

He set the cutting board with bread slices in the middle of the table, and then the bottle opener. After that, he couldn't avoid anymore looking at the notebook she held. But looking at the notebook made it tough to keep a grasp on the story he told himself about proving his family wrong.

"It's fine." He moved the rest of his school shit to the spare chair. "Beer okay, or do you want something else?"

"Hey." Leyla snagged his wrist. "I'm not judging. This is just us. Two people in beach-worn t-shirts and silly boxers. Leave your family outside the room and think about if you want help from someone who happens to be a highly recommended science and writing tutor, and who is offering because she cares about you? And also because she kind of likes talking about how to develop an assessment plan for an environmental case study?"

The fucking thing was, some part of his brain knew she'd see his assignment left out on the table. And also, she'd see the hash he was making out of it. Damn science requirement.

And that background part of his brain got all shriveled sickly green when the intrusive parental-type thoughts cheered that he'd gotten exactly the outcome they'd all like best: Leyla showing up to talk him through his confusion and mess.

He squeezed his eyes shut. Concentrated on the slim warm fingers resting on his pulse point. Let his brain weasels fuck back off into hiding while he slowed his breathing. Inhaled the aromas of warm bread and savory vegetables and Leyla's coconut saltiness.

Once his heart settled back into place, he smiled open his eyes and wrapped her into a kiss. "You caring about me is the most amazing thing that's happened in years. Thank you. And, yes, please on the assignment help. But not until after I feed you. That's more important than my classwork."

Her arms fit perfectly, circling around his back. She leaned into him. "Are you suggesting there's something besides that case study that'll require my energy tonight?"

"If at all possible. You didn't think I plastered ponies all over my junk hoping you'd ignore it, did you?"

Chapter Twenty-Five

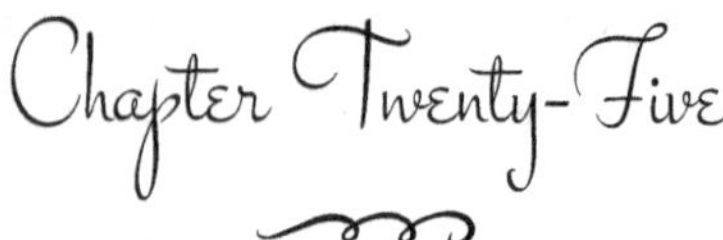

Dean Tyler messaged her to stop by his office.

"So what's that mean? He's got more to say to me then he can convey before the committee meeting?" she asked Sally. "And by the way, the committee shot down the idea of having time-based metrics."

"This is my shocked face," Sally said.

"Yeah, I know, but I did wonder if anything might come of it, instead of it being performative make work and band-aid solutions."

"You did? That was optimistic of you."

"Ha, ha. If you're going to Voice of Experience at me, what do you think Tyler wants? Because Dunlavy said they were going to send offer letters this week, and you know I've been checking all my emails and my campus mailbox twice a day."

"Well, they're not going to go through Tyler to offer you the job. They'll call you or email."

Leyla slumped back and rubbed her forehead. "I know. I don't like it."

"That's cause they haven't told you yes yet. You'll like it plenty once they do."

"If they do."

Sally fixed her with a stare. "Once they do. No way you're losing this job."

She clenched her jaw, because the one way she could lose the job was the same way she could lose control of the committee objectives and lose control of her lab time and lose control of her free time. Chad.

"Well, speculating's not going to answer your questions. Get out of here and text me later."

"Okay okay, Mama," she said, kissing Sally's cheek then using her thumb to wipe the gloss away like the auntie in training she was.

And then she marched across campus like she was girding herself for battle.

As soon as the dean's message came through, she'd pulled her life plan up on the big monitor. Everything was on point.

Coursework completed.

Excellent grades.

Three more papers authored or co-authored than she'd initially targeted.

The only Master's candidate invited to present a poster at the PacCOAST colloquium last fall—which balanced off the fact she hadn't sat on as many panels as she'd hoped.

She added a line for the podcast interview about red alga and popped it onto the her digital CV, as well. Just in case Dunlavy was reviewing those one more time before making her the offer.

She checked her in-boxes while she waited on a student to leave Dean Tyler's office. Sales junk, a couple job search alerts that featured positions she was either too new or too educated for, Zora's graduation flight info. Lance's, too, so that was how things worked now. Something to get used to.

Nothing from Dunlavy, not even one of their newsletters she felt too superstitious to unsubscribe from, in case it somehow persuaded her SMTP server to treat her job offer as spam.

"Leyla!"

As always, Tyler sounded like the sight of her reminded him what a genius he was to have her in the program.

"Morning, Dean."

"Come on in. Want to shut the door?"

Well, that was fucking ominous, as Austin would say.

The thought of him steadied her in some silly kind of way. She wasn't sure how to feel about that, but it wasn't anything she'd contemplate until she was well away from the Sciences building.

They got discursive, as usual, about whatever parts of her life Tyler could pry out of her. She kept it to university life, but that still let him range across topics like her teaching load, her capstone presentation—he beamed over her preview of Quinn's graphics—and the DEIA Action Plan review committee.

And he never brought up her internship or Dunlavy Institute once, which was a whole slew of suspiciousness.

"Do you know anyone over at Ocean Equity Partnerships?"

Her qualms ratcheted higher. "I've met Dr. Lang a few times." Nice woman, brilliant, but her organization's mission was focused on social equity in planning climate adaptations. Important and all, but not her focus.

"Excellent. They emailed this morning. Oh, so did your friend from the city council, about the Surfside Swell Expo. Wonderful work, bringing that information to us. We're putting together a partnership proposal there."

Typical Dean Tyler communication style. Roundabout and roundabout and then a cutback to something different.

And all the while, the very real possibility of tumbling under a monster wave coming up behind her.

She rolled with the subject change, and updated him about the work Sofia and Ty were putting together for their students, passing along their contact info and dropping a couple of hints about Austin's podcast, which would give the university more of their coveted positive exposure.

Thinking about Austin twice in one meeting. Maybe the man was becoming her superpower for surviving unwelcome meetings.

Dangerous. But she'd spent enough time on the ocean to understand how to recognize dangers and accept what came her way, whether it was a worrying dependence on some man or the increasing odds that Dean Tyler wanted to rope her into another project that didn't dovetail with her life plan.

Sure enough, he jumped in with a spiel about the importance of engaging disadvantaged communities in resilient solutions. Which was hardly news to anyone about to finish their Masters in Coastal Science and Policy. Still, she nodded along until he dropped his bomb, which he clearly thought of as presenting her with a bouquet.

"Dr. Lang's team created a new position. They want an equity scientist to synthesize pre-existing vulnerability assessments of coastal-dependent communities along the Californian use-area and develop adaptive climate solutions. I thought of you right away, and after what you've shown me of your capstone graphics, I'm that much more convinced you're the right candidate for the job."

Breathe in. Breathe out. Smile so he knows she's grateful. "That's amazing, Dean. Thanks for thinking of me. And I'd love to know more about what they have in mind, so please do send that information on to me."

"I sense hesitation?"

Listen to him, so proud of himself for picking up that she wasn't jumping for joy.

"It's nothing against Ocean Equity. I admire their work. But as we've discussed, I've always been primarily interested in developing scalable marine climate solutions working with government and corporate stakeholders. I want to see institutional changes. NGOs working with smaller scale fisheries and raising climate awareness among individuals and communities —of course we can't do without those groups. But my ambitions when you helped place me at Dunlavy for the summer internship haven't changed. I—we—targeted them because they're exactly where I want to start my career after graduating."

She settled herself in her chair, hoping despite everything that he would jump in and affirm everything she was saying. Instead, he glanced at his computer and blinked.

She forced herself to go on. "Dunlavy is sending their offer letters this week. So, I'll look at Ocean Equity, of course. But my first choice, the job I'll jump on, is the Dunlavy Institute."

He'd never seen Leyla so stressed. Driven, yes. Busy, for sure. Irritable, even.

But like a lot of dedicated surfers, she often seemed to release her stress into the waves. Until now, when she was pacing around the fire ring, hardly cognizant of the sun setting over the Pacific, or the music drifting up from his sister's guitar, or his attempts to hand her a drink.

Sally wandered up, snagging the beer from him and rounding Leyla up for a walk out to the waves. He hung back, watching, which was contrary to all the impulses he had.

Not the first time he'd fought his impulses. Not even the first time that day. But one of the lessons he'd had trouble accepting—okay, one he had to put front and center in his mind repeatedly over the course of his life—was this: not all his impulses were bad. And controlling them wasn't the same as outright quashing every one of them.

Since the most common outcome, all his life, when he followed his impulses was some kind of redirection or reprimand, it got to be too easy to see his impulses as something to avoid. To always do the opposite, or to counter them with restorative action, or to just sit on them until someone who wasn't him could make a judgment call.

But it turned out that everyone had impulses. And acting on them didn't constantly land all those other people in hot water or a disaster zone. He had to learn to trust that at least some of his impulses were okay. Were great, even.

And the one pushing him to jog across the sand to where Leyla and Sally huddled in conversation?

Turned out to be great, actually. Because when he reached them, Leyla snugged herself under his arm and rested her head on his shoulder and sighed like, in holding him, she'd finally let something go.

"Hey." He shifted a bit to shield her from the offshore wind, and settled in to listen.

They were hashing and rehashing a conversation with her adviser guy. Something about the wrong kind of job offer. He couldn't figure it out, so he waited until he got a chance to ask more.

See? Control, not quash.

"I fucked myself over."

"You didn't." Sally was swift, but he'd heard her more assured.

"You think before I sought out a position on the damn action plan committee, he'd have thought of me for this job? You think before he saw how Quinn's work made mine look pretty he'd have pinned me as the perfect someone to synthesize goddamn assessments they already ran without my even getting a hand in how they're crafted and collected?"

Control, control, hold her and control. *Don't jump in looking for reassurance his recommendations didn't mess up her career.*" It's a bad fit for you?"

"It's networking and data entry on somebody else's climate science. I'm not opposed to it as, like, a thing that exists. I'm opposed to getting pigeonholed into a job where my primary strengths are that I'm a woman and good optics for fundraising."

He nodded. Someone as clever and educated as Leyla ought to have a career that was the one she'd been building towards all along. He knew it wasn't that simple. Too many people he'd met ended up in jobs that didn't match the grind they put in to earn their degrees to start with. Not that he could mention that to his folks. To them, all the experience he had from working in the apartment his whole life and earning money in any number of other short-term gigs and starting up a successful business with his siblings didn't add up to the clout of a piece of paper.

But look at his sister. Even though now Pier Three seemed to be an answer to what she'd been looking for when the other job was unsustainable, she'd lived with misogyny and worse just trying to build her career. And she'd have continued facing all that shit if their Granny hadn't left them all that money they decided to use to start the coffee shop.

And his latest round of barista interviews, he'd had his choice of resumes featuring college degrees. The job was not what they dreamed of, but people had education loans and rent to pay, so they'd have taken it if he hadn't hired Elmer.

He wanted Leyla's dreams to work out for her, with no make-work required. "When you get the Dunlavy job, does this problem go away?"

Leyla grabbed the beer from Sally and drained the rest of

it. "That's the total hell of all this. It's Friday night, no offer in sight, and I wouldn't put it past Tyler to have stuck his oar in. The way he looks at it, if Chad is at Dunlavy and I'm at Ocean Equity, he's helped place two of his graduates in careers in their field and strengthened the ties between the university and the institutions. Never mind the reality of my career wiping out in a shore break before it even got started."

Chapter Twenty-Six

Ranting wasn't her usual style, but Sally and Austin didn't stop her, so fine, she was gonna rant. About Dean Tyler regarding any placement in their career field as a success, instead of caring about the applicant's personal goals. About her ire that he didn't 'right away' think of any of the equity-focused people in her cohort for the job, maybe because all of them were white. Come to that, why didn't he right away think of Jenni, when everything Jenni had done for two years, including her capstone project, all exhibited her consistent focus on low-income ocean-dependent communities? Jenni would jump at the chance to be OEP's equity scientist, and first thing she was doing when she was home was gonna be to forward the email to her. Which she wasn't going to regret, because if Jenni could get that job, she'd fly with it, and Dean Tyler wasn't as good at networking as he thought if he hadn't put Jenni and Dr. Lang together in the first place.

But if she, Leyla, took it? Would she grow into the position she wanted? No, she would not. Not at OEP, not unless they totally changed their entire focus. So: no. Which meant she'd end up leaving OEP with a resume full of donor-facing events and graphic-filled presentations and the challenge of asking a new employer to look past all that to see her for the work she could do when there wasn't a pretty slide deck in sight.

Austin hissed in a short breath.

She blew out a long one. "I'm not mad about my pretty slide decks."

In the twilight dim it was easier to hear his wry smile than to see it. "I wouldn't be bothered if you were. Anyway, you don't need to be. I'm able to be mad about them without your buy-in."

"Well, don't tell Quinn that."

"Of course I wouldn't. And I'm mad at me, not at them. It's my weird-wired brain that made you even question if the amazing hard science you worked on was good enough without a pretty slide deck."

"Austin—"

"No, never mind. It's not about me. I'm sorry for my part in contributing to what's going on now, and I won't even tease you about how you're the one trying to downplay it now. What's the best thing for you now? Tonight?"

Sally reached over to squeeze her forearm. "Good question. We bailing from here? Or instigating a dance party around the flames? Throwing down? Or are you about to let me know, ever so sweetly, that I am surplus to requirements and you're about to sneak off with Austin and his very talented tongue?"

Austin's whole body jolted at that, and he backed from her so quickly she heard him stumble into the surf.

She and Sally had to hold each other up for all their stumbling, laughing way back to the bonfire.

She muttered her apology to him when he plopped himself on the blanket beside her, but since she also pulled a smirking face at Sally, he still found himself strangely shy about joining in the crowd dynamics.

Abraham and Callie arrived then, which gave him a second to duck his head and dig through his brother's backpack for the set of flip flops he always carried. Sure, he packed them for himself, in case he ended up in the ocean, but that didn't mean Austin wasn't going to take advantage when he was the one with wet socks.

"Hey, these are mine," Austin said, yanking board shorts out of Abraham's backpack. He backed a few feet from the fire's light and dropped his work pants into the same pile as his damp socks and shoes, pulling the board shorts up over his boxers.

Abraham sniggered when he rejoined the group, which he was sure had everything to do with the glow-in-the-dark banana boxers he was wearing, and not because he'd noticed the way Sally was teasing Leyla about their sex life.

He snagged a beer. It seemed like a necessary part of coming to understand why Sally's tongue teasing set him on edge. He couldn't right away see how it was different from everyone ribbing him about his crush on Leyla. Plenty of those jokes came with the implication that his primary desire was sex with the woman. No one had let up on their comments about his being ecstatic that Leyla finally gave him a chance, and those jokes were fine.

Observational humor, full of nothing but the truth.

So was he just being a prude, offended that Leyla must have made some comment about his excellent cunnilingus skills? Or was it something more?

He settled in to think, blocking out the goings on around them and probing for the sore spots that were clues to understanding his emotions.

It wasn't Leyla's tongue-wagging goofing. That was near the emotional bruise, but not on it. Yes, he'd nearly fallen in the water when Sally referenced their sex life, but part of that had been clowning in an effort to make Leyla laugh.

Okay, a lot of it was to make her laugh. It wasn't the first time he'd played the clown with her. Not even the first time since they started dating. It was a go-to move for him. And he'd learned that it was a trick he used to make people like him, when he was worried he brought too much chaos to the table.

Thinking too much about that always left him feeling like his soul had a hollow glass tube rammed through it where other people were full of genuine connection. But that was nothing new, so be shoved it aside and kept thinking.

He'd had an eight-hour shift before closing at the cafe, meaning he'd walked straight from work to the fire pit where his friends gathered on Friday nights. He'd kept a lookout for Leyla as soon as he got there. During work hours, she'd texted a bit about her meeting with the dean, and he hadn't realized how much it had shaken her.

Fuck's sake, she'd let him pepper her with questions about the Surfside Swell Expo and what they needed to tell Mateo. While all along she was dealing with the ramifications of the guy she relied on to facilitate her professional connections misreading her entire life plan. He wished she'd have shared that with him. Or that he could go back in time and figure it out himself, so she wouldn't have to turn to Sally for comfort.

He was rubbing the base of his palm into his sternum before his thoughts caught up to what his body was doing.

That was it.

That was the bruise.

And hell if it wasn't a deep one.

Leyla wasn't setting out on purpose to inform him that she liked him for his goofball nature and for sex. Which was fine. He was thrilled to be able to tease with her, and fuck with her.

But when she'd arrived at the bonfire, she didn't even try to unload on him about her problems.

She'd gone straight to Sally. They'd stepped off together to talk it out. Leyla was grappling with big issues. Things that spoke to her soul. She showed up to seek out support, and he was right there.

But it wasn't Good Time Austin that she reached for.

Chapter Twenty-Seven

Sally handed over her phone. "Look at this."

"Why are you following Chad?"

"Baby, I keep my enemies close."

Leyla's smile stopped fast when she read what he'd posted. She shoved the phone at Sally and turned to Austin, who'd been quietly nursing his beer. "Can we go?"

He handed his drink across to his brother and stood with a smile. "At your service."

Something was off in stance, but her need to be away from people overrode anything else. "Good. Great."

"I take it you don't mind coming to my place?" He stooped to grab his damp work clothes.

"No. That's exactly where I want to go." She took his hand as they navigated across the sand to the Pier Three parking lot. It earned them a couple of wolf-whistles and a loud, "Good night!" from Abraham. She glanced over her shoulder to see Sally leaning in close conversation with Noah, so it seemed like everyone would know the news soon enough.

It burst from her as soon as they were in the car. "Chad got the Dunlavy job."

"He what?" Austin shook his head. "I mean, I heard you, but how is that possible?"

"He posted it. A screenshot and everything: 'Dear Chad we are pleased to offer' blah blah blah."

"Leyla. Shit. That ... that just sucks."

She nodded. The venom in her brain jiggled around with the motion, so she sank against the headrest. "It totally sucks."

"I'm sorry. Want to talk it through? Want a hug? How can I help?"

His touch was gentle, and she didn't want that. Anything tender and she'd shatter, and fucking Chad wasn't allowed the power to make her shatter.

She gripped his hand and pulled it to her lap. Pressed hard. "I only want you to take me home and take my mind off everything."

Austin slipped his hand away to start the car. "Sure thing, Leyla. Anything you need."

He performed to her expectations. Lifted her into a passionate kiss against the door as soon as they got inside; shifted to hitch her onto the kitchen counter and slowly, with light teasing touches and plenty of dirty talk, stripped off her shirt. Turned all of his devotion to her breasts. Buried his head into the valley between them and licked and nipped at the flesh above her bra cups, all the while gently thumbing her hardening nipples. Wedged himself inside her thighs so she could rock intently, then jolt hard against him when he snapped her bra straps.

Her cry was inarticulate, but she grabbed his face and asked, "What was that?"

"Too much?"

She found his balls and squeezed. "Too much?"

"Not even."

"Exactly. Carry on."

He didn't do it again, because the fun was when she wasn't expecting it. Instead he lifted her breast out of the cup and went to work laving and sucking her nipple to a diamond point. The other cup, he left in place, tracing the lower swell back and forth, back and forth, but never touching so much as the areola. Her gyrations were getting wilder and wilder, and when he suddenly switched the suck the other nipple, hard, through the satin of the bra, Leyla cried out and gripped his hair.

Moments later, he had her naked, and ripped off his own shirt while guiding her to the couch. People laughed at his setup, big couch and storage ottomans and no tables or anything, but he didn't have to navigate through any fragile shit before he was kneeling in front of her and spreading her legs wide.

"Austin," she said, and that was all, but he loved the neediness in her voice. He loved the way she opened herself to him. He loved that dawn patrol scent driving him wilder for her.

Getting lost in Leyla's need for him was almost—almost— a balm.

Curling one finger, and then a second, into her, he bit down on her inner thigh and sucked hard, suddenly desperate to leave a mark on her. Desperate for her to feel him, even a little, past this night. Desperate for so much more. So much he wasn't going to name, because all Leyla wanted from him was for him to tease her g-spot and for him to amp up her excitement and for him to unleash his goddamn tongue on her.

He did. He held her hips in place while he lipped her slit, and pulsed the flat of his tongue to her clit, and did all those things she expected of him. Even a couple she didn't expect, but didn't mind at all, given how she yanked his hair and bucked into his mouth and pulled him over her so he could, at last, at least, sink into her and kiss her and hold her and watch her as she met his thrusts with an abandonment that proved to him that he was giving her exactly what she needed.

"All that and we didn't even make it to the bedroom."

"Well," he huffed, still catching his breath.

She twirled her fingers through his hair, mussing and smoothing and mussing again. "Thanks, babe."

He hummed something interrogatory, sliding to take a little weight off her.

"That was just what I needed." She'd been vibrating with a toxic stew of anger and disappointment and insecurity, but Austin had a way of bringing her into the present. Not only with his superior sexing skills, not that she was ever going to object to those. But somehow by being himself—by his take life where it is attitude, by his ability to see something promising in every situation. The more time she spent with him, the more settled she felt.

And these moments. The ones when they were breathing in sync, hearts full from coming together, and a golden current buzzed quietly between them.

She could definitely come to rely on moments like these.

Only problem was, the longer they lay there, her heart relaxing and her body following suit, the more obvious it was that he was not in sync with her. It was a dismal change from how they'd been in the past. Something was off. She waited to see if he would disclose ... something—some sort of reciprocity or gratitude or parity, or she didn't know what—in balance with the things she'd taken upon herself to tell him that night.

She'd spent all day with Austin on her mind, deep in her heart, even on her phone screen. And now in her presence. But instead of responding by telling her what was keeping him keyed up, he was pretending things were normal.

Chapter Twenty-Eight

"So, what is it?"

He squeezed her fingers and asked, "What's what?" with the most obviously over-cheerful tone she'd ever heard. Not even when he was defusing an entitled customer did he sound so goddamn affable and approachable.

"'What's what?'" She pulled back a bit to glare at him.

Because step one was acting like things were fine when they weren't. But she was not getting into a two-step of straight up denial. That was now how she danced through this world.

He stayed quiet, so she said, "You aren't about to lay there and tell me nothing's going on with you?"

"I am saying there's nothing going on," he deadpanned.

"Yeah, suddenly, for the first time in your life, you have an orgasm and it doesn't reduce your tension? Call me suspicious if you like, but I'm not buying it."

"Fine, I'm calling you suspicious."

"Austin. Come on." She pushed him to sit up and grabbed for her clothes. "This is ridiculous. Don't be willful and obstinate with me, please. I've spent all day navigating guys trying to be clever at me with their avoidance words, and I'm not up for doing the same with you."

"I never asked you to navigate anything with me, Leyla. All I've done is show up when you wanted me, and done exactly what you asked. And now that I have, you're still mad at the world or something, so you're all microanalytical on how I breathe? Should I get started on round two so you can get more out of your system?"

Oh, he did not just say that. She could not be required to deal with this level of petulance after the day she'd had.

"Babe, those orgasms were nice and all, but they don't make up for the fact that I just lost the exact job I've been working towards for half my life. Ain't nobody's penis that magic."

He stomped to his room and returned with a fresh shirt and boxers. The mood she was in, she wasn't even checking to see what was printed on them.

He had a mood of his own, apparently. "Fine. It seems we can admit that you're feeling a bit of a mess because of the job, but not that you only turned to me when you needed a convenient form of stress relief? That I'm not good enough to talk to you about it?"

All the air in her body was lodged only up in her sternum, and she didn't know how to force it to circulate. "I think you'd better explained that last statement."

He had the gall to cross his arms at her. "I think it speaks for itself, but fine. What I'm saying in so many words is when something's going on with me, when I'm stressed or worried or, hell, if I'm happy as fuck, you're the one I'm telling about it. I'm turning to you and saying 'hey, Leyla. This is me, splayed open. It's who I am, and what's important to me is to share that with you.'"

"You're standing there with your arms closed tight like you always do when you're afraid of being too needy, and talking about being wide open to me? You're accusing me of being closed off just 'cause I don't splay the exact same way you do?" So much for all those times she had Austin with her all day. So much for thinking of him as a bulwark. So much for thinking how he'd shown her new ways to consider her situation. "When Sally showed me that post from Chad, the first thing I did was turn to you."

"First thing you did was turn to me so we can fuck. That's not the same thing, Leyla, and you know it." He was fully bitter with her now.

Her emotions flew over the dam she was trying to hold them behind. "Well, shit, I'm sorry I'm not expressing myself exactly like you would. Didn't we have this conversation sixteen times? You know you're different—"

"Different to everyone. Yeah, I get it. I'm the odd one. And no one could be expected to have any desire to interact with me, no matter how much I've come to depend on them."

"I have every desire to interact with you." Her arms waved between them almost of their own accord, but what did he think 'can we go to your place' was about if not interacting with him?

"Didn't seem that way when you were telling Sally all the details of your day, and I was only good for handing over a beer and warming your back."

"Hold up. You want me to cut off Sally because you're in the picture now?"

"Gah. Obviously not."

"There's nothing obvious about it, Austin. It's what I'm piecing together from the way you're acting. You're in your man-baby feelings that I asked you to take my mind off it."

"I'm saying, you weren't taking your mind off it when you were talking to Sally at the bonfire. You went to her and told her what was going on. Walked right past me to do it, too. We were fourteen inches from each other, Leyla, and you ignored me and went off with her."

She had jelly legs. It was worse than her first day of her first surf camp, practicing pop-ups on the sand over and fucking over again before she could get anywhere near the waves. She wasn't going to sit back down on his accursed couch, so she yanked out a dining room chair and sank into it.

"All I'm hearing is that you don't think my way of turning to you is good enough. I haven't written your name in sharpie on Rainbow's rails or whatever, so when I turn to you with this genuine need like I did? Because don't twist it, Austin. Did I want to bang out a little stress relief? Sure. That's not so unique a response to my situation. But it's also no proof that I wasn't turning to you, specifically, with all the volatile emotions in my heart. I'm not talking about how you have your unique way of thinking. I'm talking about how I—*me*, and go ahead and call me selfish for being mainly concerned with myself tonight—process emotions and setbacks and the complete goddamn devastation of everything I've been working for."

She turned from him, because it was no good letting him see her face crumble. Not if had no interest in helping her survive this fucking disaster of a situation. "You know what? I don't need to tell you all this. Not if all you're gonna do is compare how I act with you—who I thought was my new boyfriend—to how I act with someone who's been with me literally every step since I moved to Surfside."

"I am your boyfriend."

He didn't move any closer, didn't take back his complaints about her not needing him in the right way. Didn't rub her shoulders and pour her a glass of wine and carry her to cuddle in bed where she could pretend she wasn't going to cry about losing Dunlavy and getting sidelined by Tyler.

She gathered her breath and let it fly. "Austin, tell me

something. Was today the worst day of your professional life? Were you dicked around by someone you thought you could trust, and overlooked by an institution you thought would value you? Was the person who spent the past two years piggy-backing on your work and claiming it—actually naming it—as his own, given the opportunity he only even knew about because he was lurking every time you talked about your goals?" She didn't turn around to see if he was nodding or shaking his head or in any way acknowledging her.

He damn sure wasn't saying, "You know what, Leyla? You have a point, that was a lot of crap to happen today and you should get to handle it however is best for you." That glass of wine was nowhere on offer.

She snorted, and sniffled because she wasn't in the right state to snort without snot. "Yeah, I didn't think so. Maybe if you're as dedicated to me and this relationship as you claim, you can try being fine with how I process this shit day. Maybe act like you're supportive of me, instead of whatever this is. This acting like not only do I not have the right to handle things in a way I know works for me, but I also have to be responsible for your feelings on the matter? And while you're at it, maybe you can learn the difference between being that open book you claim you are, and being resilient enough to meet me where I am. Go look up the ring theory of support in your communications texts, will you? Once you've read up on that, here's an idea: make a plan to not pout about me relying on you wrong, until sometime *after* I'm done actually needing that support. After that, I promise, I'll take all the time you need to manage you being butthurt."

Chapter Twenty-Nine

Being told she felt she had to manage him?

That was it for him.

He snagged his discarded board shorts, shuffled into Abe's flip flops, and headed out. The elevator was on the ground level so he closed himself in the box before making his clothes and hair tidy on the ride to the top floor.

He sank down outside Mom and Dad's door. They were home; he could hear them moving around in there. But he wasn't in the mood to be in front of anyone.

He'd grabbed his phone but left his keys in case she wanted to drive herself home. It would only take one text for Abraham to come by and let him back into his apartment. Or he could knock on his parents' door and borrow their spare key. He didn't need to figure any of that out just yet.

He just needed to be away from Leyla.

Anyway, if he contacted anyone in his family, they'd instantly go into babying Austin mode. Telling him he wasn't really ready to live his own life. Telling him was too immature to be in a relationship.

Leyla had made that point perfectly well and his family did not need to pile on.

He messaged her about taking his car, then muted her. May as well put his fingers in his ears and chant nonsense so no one could speak to him. It was just as useless at keeping him from wondering what she was going to say to him next.

There was nothing to scroll on, nothing to reply to, nothing to watch, nothing to distract him from her words.

The orgasms were nice and all, but
Not dedicated to this relationship
I also have to be responsible for you

The way her shoulders had hunched in. The way he'd failed to hold her to him.

I thought you were my new boyfriend
Your man-baby feelings

And how her voice pitched all over the place.

Manage you being butthurt

Every phrase was more proof that she'd finally figured out she was too good for him. She didn't have to parrot exactly his family's words for him to make the connection: she agreed that he wasn't worth taking as he was. If he was different, if he'd managed to grow up as much as he pretended he had, if he could even get the most basic degree without turning to her for help. If he wasn't always a fuckup.

And what the hell did it matter? He'd loved her from afar for ages. He could go back to it.

Just because now he knew her intimately, knew how much more worthy and funny-sly and brilliant and important and sexy she was than he'd gleaned from across the bonfire. From across the barista counter. From across all the barriers reinforcing how she was a shining genius who would save the planet, and he was just a dropout who'd only made it anywhere in life because his family took pity on him.

None of that would stop him from loving her from afar

forever. Would it make it hurt a thousand percent more? Sure, but it wouldn't stop him for being as stuck in perpetual longing as he'd been before.

She hadn't responded.

He took her off mute and stared at the phone, in case it was hiding her message from him.

It wasn't. Two minutes, and then three. Nothing. She'd made herself clear: she was done humoring him. He'd failed to show up for her when her heart was shattered, and compounded it by realizing—even while he could scent her on his skin—that his failures were exactly what everyone always told him they were.

And now he was the shattered one, because being with her one second more, forcing her to name all his flaws in case he was unaware of them, wasn't something he could do.

Instead, he'd run away, a coward and a fool. Even turning around and going back now, chasing her to her apartment, sending apology bouquets, anything would be too late. His inadequacies were too front and center for her to forgive or let slide.

The stubbornly blank phone screen only showed him his red-rimmed eyes and bleak-ass face. So maybe that's why his father looked worried, when the door opened, to find him blinking and slumped against the opposite wall.

"Austin. Honey, are you okay?"

"Dad. Hi." He scrubbed at his face and pushed himself to stand.

"What's going on? Come in."

Shaking his head, Austin groped behind him for the elevator call button. "I'm heading out. I only came up here to tell you I quit."

"You need a bubble bath or something," Zora said when Leyla finished relaying all the evil entirety of her day. "Want me to find you a hotel with a tub for tonight? It's on me."

"And me," Lance added, from close enough that Leyla heard it without her sister's speakerphone being on. So that was humiliating.

May as well compound it. "Austin's got a tub; I could use it."

Silence.

More silence.

Enough silence that she checked they hadn't been cut off.

Finally: "Leyla."

"Zora."

"Leyla Robinson, are you conveying to me the extremely troubling information that you are still in that man-child's apartment?"

She sniffed. "He said I could take his car. But I don't want to leave him stranded."

"Baby, he walked out. Middle of a fight. Walked."

"I know—"

"Out. Walked. Out."

Leyla forced herself to look around Austin's apartment. The living room focused on his gaming system. The one corner bookcase full of family photos and a random-seeming collection of bobble-heads, shot glasses, and board games. An assortment of used sticky notes folded into frogs, hearts, boats, fish, and, of course, butterflies. His shabby stuffed elephant.

All the sparks of his personality huddled in the margins. He spent so much time making space for her—for everyone— but almost erased himself from his own home. She wondered what it had looked like before his brother moved out.

"Leyla."

"I know. I know he did." She sighed. "Not sure that means I'm going to do the same."

"Leyla." Zora was channeling their mom at her most 'I'm not mad, I'm disappointed.'

"I know." Her mouth was cotton. She fetched herself a beer. "Maybe I'll leave, I don't know yet. I keep coming back to the fact that the fight started 'cause I couldn't leave well enough alone. If I hadn't pressed him to say—"

"No. Nope. That was you being sensitive to his needs. A thing, let's remember, he didn't do for you. Or stopped doing, the second you didn't go along with him feeling sorry for himself when you didn't replace your best friend with him."

"It wasn't quite that."

"Wasn't it?"

She drank. Wandered into his dreamy new bathroom, all green and underwater feeling, somehow. Not quite like being in the barrel, but reminiscent of that same peace and euphoria. A space where Austin was finally asserting himself. "Oh, shit."

"Oh shit what? Is he back? Are you okay?"

Her arm shook a little as she set the beer bottle on the counter and stepped into the bathtub. Any hope she'd been mistaken dissolved when she picked up the new bottle there. "He bought my conditioner."

More and more silence. Then, quietly: "Oh, Leyla."

She didn't need more of her sister's urging. She'd already gathered up the rest of her shit and opened her ride share app on the way to the lobby. No way was she currently able to abide any more face-to-face encounters with Austin Wells.

Chapter Thirty

"Do you need a hug?"

He glared at his sister. "Why would I need a hug?"

"So the rumor is true."

He flinched and Alicia nodded, which was incredibly rude of her.

"Fine, you don't want to talk about it. One thing, though."

He scooped some Kona blend into the grinder in hopes of drowning out whatever she was going to say.

Instead, she just moved closer into his space. "Remember: our partnership agreement isn't like your at-will employment with Mom and Dad. If you're planning to abandon us, there are some very specific steps you have to take. I'm not going to tell you what they are, either. You'll have to figure them out on your own."

He abandoned the grinder and ducked his head. His shoulders were shaking and something unidentifiable between a laugh and a sob hiccuped out of him.

Alicia wrapped him in a tight hug. It was one of the best ways she was like Dad: her instant and fierce enfolding of him.

She muttered something and guided him to the office, positioning herself in the doorway to keep an eye on the café while shielding him from everyone else.

"So, this isn't about your jobs?" she asked.

Which he would have thought was perfectly clear, but maybe it was her way of being gentle. She also handed over a pile of napkins, so, yeah, he shouldn't be so cynical about his hard-nosed sister showing a tender side.

"Is it Leyla?"

He didn't answer. No need to address the obvious. Instead, he wiped at his eyes and blew his nose.

Licie waited him out. It was one of the annoying ways she was like Dad. The man had practically planted himself in Austin's apartment after he retrieved his spare key, watching him pace around as if after three or four thousand tight circles around the living room, Austin would cave and talk more.

Maybe all those steps he'd taken the night before, and the way he'd reeled when he saw where Leyla had left her beer in the bathroom next to the product he'd bought for her, plus the pedaling to get himself to Pier Three that morning, all added up. Or maybe this was one of those situations when a sibling was more palatable to cry at than a parent.

Whatever it was, he started blabbing. "I fucked up. She needed me and I—she called it dealing with my butthurt feelings. I made it about me."

"Oh, Austin."

"I know. I *know*! I'm an ass. So now I'm screwed."

"Well, what did she say? You apologized, right?"

He balled up all his gross napkins and shoved them in the nearly full office trash can. Then he untied the liner and started to pull it free.

"Austin?"

He was so done with sharing time. He shoved past her

with the trash bag, slamming his shoulder into the fire door on his way to the dumpster.

It wasn't satisfyingly bang-y enough, so he stomped up the stairs to the conference suite. No one else was on shift in the cafe, meaning Alicia would be stuck downstairs monitoring the counter.

He tamed his overlarge motions and slipped into the empty recording booth and called up the files he had on his podcast.

Maybe he sucked at supportive relationships, and maybe he was no good as Leyla's partner, but she believed in his ideas for Surfside Swell. She somehow thought he was capable of finishing his degree. Of accomplishing one goddamn thing in his life, even though it was hard.

No, that wasn't what he'd learned from her. He would get the degree *because* it was hard.

Talking about that with her had been one of those moments of learning how he wanted his life to go while he was in the process of speaking it. But instead of taking that initial thought and talking past it until he'd negated his initial concept, Leyla had stopped him. Forced him to sit with the idea. To let enough light in around the edges that it could develop into something shiny to brighten up his mind.

It wasn't like he'd never explored ways to combat negative self-talk before. It was something about Leyla's magnetic alchemy that had helped him stick it in place.

He set his phone to flash silently at him in case Alicia messaged him for help with the customers, then dove into the final edits on the first three podcast episodes. With them complete and a couple of other interviews recorded, he had all he needed to cut together an intro reel as episode zero. He dug through all his notes until he'd triple checked he'd gotten the numbering protocol right, and uploaded the first batch of eps for the podcaster to run their quality checks. Next, they'd need social media graphics, but Ty's and Sofia's students were going to work on those. He wrote up the episode descriptions as an email, along with photos they'd captured during then interviews, to send to the relevant people.

It had to go to Quinn, to add to the website. Ty and Sofia to get their students busy. Mateo, as a heads-up on what they were doing. And Leyla.

He deleted and re-added her email three times before he forced himself to hit send with her included. If he'd completed the work before their fight—he knew this was the logic his brother would advise—he'd have copied her. So, it was wrong to cut her out just because he was feeling precious about his miserable heart.

Such a crap weekend.

Leading into it with Friday, the Day of Doom to all her Desires, was no help. But then her laptop crashed before she'd saved some of the fiddly work she'd done on her capstone. And Lance sent her tulips, which was nothing but a reminder that her sister had found a fabulous-for-her man who seemed intent on leapfrogging into a sibling relationship with her. And there was that email from Austin. And her roommate asked if she could use the last of the butter, which seemed fine when she said yes but only meant she craved toast all afternoon. And then it rained all Sunday and the ocean was a mess so she didn't get to surf.

And again, nothing but that one damn generic cc: email from Austin.

Not that she reached out, either. Because why should she? Was it her job to make him stop running away from her? To tell him he was about to fire-bomb their whole relationship? To point out her love was more valuable than his snit?

Nope. She was done with tutoring people. He could learn all that on his own.

Soggy from multiple treks with groceries from the parking lot to her kitchen, she wrapped herself in her favorite robe and retreated to deal with her hair. Two hours of binging shows with no other demands on her mind or her body or her heart than the familiar rituals of washing, detangling, conditioning, and styling. She could bear that.

She cued up *Point Break*, deciding Johnny Utah was who she needed. Guns and waves and a chance to snark at people who thought data based-analysis was the be all and end all. Little baby Keanu getting rag dolled into love. Found families goofing off and making trouble around a beach bonfire.

Leyla missed her family.

She'd been living mostly in Surfside for six years, and they were mostly all in Phoenix. Everyone visited back and forth. She was constantly on video calls. But it wasn't the same as having everyone nearby for those circuitous conversations full of casual fondness and references to weeks past and the way Zora could raise one eyebrow and say, "Pudding," and Mom would think it was one in-joke but the sisters knew it was another. She missed her dad singing her name every time they passed in the hall. She missed shoving her cousins away because they ignored her complaints about the heat and wedged themselves shoulder-to-shoulder with her on the sofa. She missed the constant everyday touches.

And Austin.

That was the crappiest part of the whole crappy weekend. She had no room in her life for missing Austin.

Chapter Thirty-One

Suddenly it seemed like half her closest friends were part of this Surfside Swell shit.

She should have figured that out sooner. Like, before walking into the Expo planning meeting.

Thing was, Sally was the hub of so much of her social life; had been since the first time she walked into the university library as a fresh undergrad. Pals from the dorms, peers from her degrees, the people she'd met in the Black surfing community—any of the ones who stuck, all got wrapped into Sally's orbit by virtue of their proximity and her gregariousness, and meanwhile she'd gotten swirled into all of Sally's social whirls. So, by now everyone had been to bonfire; everyone went to Pier Three Coffee; everyone knew Noah's Surf Gear was the best place for unique t-shirts and afternoon parking lot concerts.

So how was she supposed to stay integrated in this community of hers, if doing so meant constantly running up against Austin and his people?

Okay, it had barely been a couple of months since their first kiss, and maybe they'd fix their shit and no one would label her as Austin's awkward, boring ex. Meanwhile, she was surrounded by his people like she'd never created a found family of her own. It was a ridiculous and also agonizing feeling, and she didn't want to live with it for as long as she lived in Surfside.

Probably she'd have to move after graduation, anyway. So at least there was a time limit on her awkward encounters. All her job searching was turning up exactly nothing local, unless she wanted to yank the OEP opportunity out from under Jenni only two days after telling her about it. And never mind how she'd watched her friend's entire self light up. Jenni had resigned herself to taking a fisheries research job up in Alaska, which, while interesting and important in its way, wasn't the right culmination of years of work for her. Same way the OEP job wouldn't be a culmination for Leyla.

Why spend her entire adult life researching and calculating the exact experience she'd need for the exact career she wanted, only to go hijacking somebody else's dreams instead? That wasn't her.

Which put her back in her grumpy place, contemplating the many, many jobs she'd have to apply for that would throw her life in directions nowhere visible on her grand goddamn plan.

She wasn't naive. She knew plenty of highly experienced people had to pivot and go with the flow of what was available, no matter how much they wanted something different. If her friends and the internet hadn't taught her that, surfing certainly had.

She wasn't greedy. She wasn't trying to demand instant success at the top of her chosen field. She'd crafted her grand plan specifically to make her an ideal entry-level coastal scientist, and not only for Dunlavy. Though, with bitter hindsight, she could see that she'd been heavily focused on becoming who they, specifically, would seek to hire.

Hell, she'd been right, too, since Chad had copied her as closely as possible and gone and gotten the job.

Plus one to her planning skills.

Minus one to the hiring committee at the Dunlavy Institute. She could almost hear them saying, "These are both excellent candidates, but there's just something—I can't put my finger on it—but it makes me lean towards him."

And, oh, what surprise they would evince should anybody suggest that if they were asked to picture a scientist, their brains would conjure up images of a white man instead of a Black woman. And, no, they didn't have to deliberately place less value on her race and gender for those ingrained biases to be at play.

Had they overcome that and looked at her and Chad dispassionately and also not taken into account his steady campaign to downplay Leyla's accomplishments? Maybe, sure. But they also hadn't treated Chad's statements as much of a mark against him. She knew his resume as well as he knew hers, and knew, too, that she'd earned higher marks, collaborated with more people, and presented more papers than him throughout their years in grad school. She was the better candidate, and he was a pale copy, and still she'd lost out to him.

So it looked like another place entirely was the ticket. Goodbye, Surfside, and all of the swellness and great local vibe and her favorite surfing beach and Austin's perfect hazelnut lattes. She'd once met somebody on a paddle-out protest who was from the Carmel area. That wouldn't be so far from her comfort zone, and she could dive right into an established community of Black surfers. As a way to pop-up on her feet, it wasn't the worst plan.

She made a note to contact that pal of Jenni's who'd gone to work at the Monterey Bay Aquarium after graduating from their program the prior year. He was a Seafood Watch Fisheries Scientist there, last she'd heard.

Again, not her preferred focus. But at least it would be a job.

"Leyla?"

Cheeks warm, she looked up from her phone to find the Expo committee—her damn friends—all sitting around the super special table Austin had saved from demolition and given a new life in the Pier Three Conference Suite. Or whatever the exalted backstory of the conference table was; she'd been paying just as little attention back when Alicia first recruited her to work on the Expo project with Austin.

Back when he was just a fidgety barista with pretty brown eyes and a flirty canine smile.

Now he was still and almost shrinking behind the crowd at the table, noticeable mostly because he was the only one not looking all expectant and curious at her.

"Sorry, what?"

Mateo cleared his throat like he'd caught her awkwardness by dint of sitting beside her. "You met with Dean Tyler last week?"

Her whole self felt like one giant unshed tear. It took her even more embarrassing moments before she separated out the few moments of her Day of Doom that had to do with the current discussion, and managed to pull the strands free enough to relay them to the crowd.

He'd told Mateo it was a bad idea for him to go.

Alicia would have used his life as dinner table conversations or whatever; Mateo already knew Leyla had no more use for him. But instead of letting her avoid him so she could shine without him making things uncomfortable, Mateo insisted on his presence.

So there they were, face to face. Sort of. She'd keep her gaze on her phone the whole time, so it was more like his face to the crown of her head. Turned out, he was perfectly capable of dissolving into longing and lust and loneliness just looking at the part of her hair.

She didn't look at him even when she lifted her gaze to address the group. Her voice was normal, and that hurt more than her broken tones from Friday night. More than her silence ever since.

At least he knew he'd brought that on himself. No way should she speak to him when he'd done nothing to regain her affection. Nothing she was aware of, anyway. Nothing she could see, react to, opt to accept or reject.

He was still too much of a mess to make an overture. But fuck if sitting there, watching her flip through her project sheets to pull up every bit of information anyone asked for, including the stuff he'd added to their effort ... it was agony. Beautiful agony, because at least they were in the same room.

But agony, because it was one thing to be a work in progress, imperfect human, like pretty much everyone. It was another entirely to inflict the disaster of his self onto someone as amazing as Leyla Robinson and hope for the best. He wasn't—could not be—the burden thrown in her lap that his family thought was his own best hope for success.

Chapter Thirty-Two

The meeting didn't take literally forever. Only nearly so. He edged towards the door while Mateo wrapped up, knowing if he was first down the stairs he could snag his bike and be a half-mile in the other direction before she made it out to head back to campus.

Abraham got a handful of his t-shirt and wouldn't let go. Damn stubborn brother. When Austin resisted being dragged towards a recording studio, Abe flashed his prosthetic, setting the fingers in a pincer grip in his ever-so-subtle reminder that his guidance could be more forceful if Austin didn't comply.

They hadn't wrestled once since his brother moved out. He fucking missed that.

Alicia followed them into the studio and shut the door. Austin looked between his siblings, both sporting the bossy looks they'd shown him a million times since he was little.

He'd researched soundproofing a lot when building the studios. The ocean was right off the building, and plenty of noise drifted up from the cafe. Not to mention discussions from the conference table. He'd opted for a floating floor and a second layer of sound-blocked sheetrock along with acoustic caulk and insulated doors. It was all really effective, but once three adults stood in the studio, two of them bent on criticizing him? The thick walls and low ceiling added to the feeling that everyone and everything was closing in on him.

He shifted to perch on the desk so he didn't feel hemmed in by siblings on either side, even though they still blocked his access to the door. He stopped conjuring up images of bad guys stopping our hero, in favor of remembering that Dad, at least, would scold them should they beat him to a pulp. Mom might even fuss at Alicia for it, too.

"What is this?" He asked like he was completely confused to be holed up in the space that used to be Alicia's kitchen, before he found new homes for all of her appliances and reformed the space in a way that profited them all.

Because he had done. They treated him like a bonehead baby brother the whole time he was coming up with the idea for the recording studios and conference suite, but had either of them had better ideas? Nope. He was the one who'd found the solution to save their business and obtain a loan to buy the property.

"We need to give some kind of profit share to the Santos's."

"What?" Alicia, at least, was derailed, which was at least part of his intent when he blurted out his latest idea.

"For Diana and Issac. They've been referring other people to the recording studios. I don't know if profit sharing is the thing I mean?" He glanced at Abraham, who knew numbers. Alicia knew numbers, too, but Abraham loved numbers. "Their dad ran this place for decades when it was a bait shop, and that was steady for him and all, but it didn't it give him much to pass down to his kids. Not like Granny did for us. Or like Mrs. Vallejo is doing for her daughter and grandkids."

Mrs. Vallejo and her husband had owned the bait shop

when it was in operation, and she was their landlord when they first converted it to Pier Three Coffee.

"I mean, I kind of see where you're coming from, but—"

Abraham interrupted Alicia. "No, it makes sense. We can't solve all the problems with the lack of generational wealth on a case by case basis, I don't think that's what he's suggesting. And the Santos siblings have directly brought in several new clients. I don't want to change our deal with the podcast network, but maybe a bounty for them individually?"

"That scheduling widget on the site was Diana's idea," Alicia said, voice all thoughtful. "She came up with the slogan, too."

Abraham pulled out his phone and typed some stuff. "I'll run some numbers and come up with a plan. And talk to Diana, too, about contracting with her for marketing."

"Hell, if Austin's gonna bail on us, we may try to hire her to manage the place." And like that, Alicia inexorably brought them all back to whatever this little confab was about to begin with.

"I told you I'm not leaving."

"No, you walked away when I suggested you were, and you've been ignoring Dad's calls."

"And my texts," Abraham added.

"None of you have said anything I need to respond to."

"That's your opinion, but it's based on some imaginary scenario where I ask questions I don't want the answers to."

"They weren't questions," he shot back at his brother. "They were accusations."

"We are not going to have a semantic debate here." Alicia butted in using her no-nonsense voice and high-profile vocabulary. "You maintain that if you were gonna leave us, you'd inform us, which thus far you haven't. So that means you're not sure. If you were sure, you'd say you're sure and set our minds at ease. And if we aren't going to be put to ease on that, there's nothing else to discuss."

Suited him. He stood.

Alicia and Abraham actually moved to stand shoulder to shoulder in front of the door, like this was an action movie after all. If it was, and if he was the hero, he'd have moves he could deploy now to overpower them and flee the scene.

Good thing it wasn't a movie, or he'd have to start calculating the odds that he was, in fact, the hero and not the villain. And unlike his sister and brother, Austin did not love numbers.

Since he didn't know how to do the math, he settled for glaring at them and repeating his initial question. "What is this?"

His siblings exchanged a look that proved they'd been talking about him behind his back, which wasn't a surprise. Abe tugged off his ball cap and scrubbed his head Licie crossed her arms. Finally, his brother huffed out a breath and asked, "What can we do to get you back together with Leyla?"

And that was the last half ounce of bile he needed to overflow his bitter steaming cup of acid. "Why? What's so important to you about me dating Leyla? How does it affect your life? Or yours? Both of you, you've got your degrees and you live with your partners and you're content with your careers. Nothing about my mess affects you one way or another. I can fail my class and destroy my relationship and quit my job—even leave this one, since you've found my replacement already—without it having one single thing to do with either of you."

"Austin," Alicia said, full of annoyance and dismay, because that was the worst way she was most like Mom. "We're not asking because of how it impacts our lives, you deliberately obtuse brat. We're asking because we love you and care about your happiness. And when things were right with Leyla, you were happy."

All the acoustic panels in the room and still her words rang through the air, echoing from all sides.

Abraham was nodding along with Alicia, but the thing he said to press in on Austin's overloaded heart was, "What class?"

Chapter Thirty-Three

Low on her personal priority list: meeting with Dean Tyler before she'd come near to recovering from how he'd blithely messed up her entire future. But she'd committed to this Surfside Swell Expo and—not to get all bitter about it—Leyla honored her responsibilities.

She went out of her way to make sure people didn't find themselves abandoned and at a loss for support.

Also, maybe she was the tiniest bit bitter, but who was going to stop her? Nobody, if the continued radio silence from Austin was any indication.

So she talked through her career situation with Sally. And Zora. And her parents. And her undergrad stats prof, who wasn't involved in any way but they'd always gotten along and he'd been a sympathetic ear in the past, in a classically avuncular way Dean Tyler could never hope to achieve.

Not that she expected any of them to give her an out, but some part of her had been hopeful of a solution that didn't mean sitting there while Dean Tyler congratulated himself on all he'd done to make her life better.

As if any facets of the most important dreams she'd always held were working out.

Grimly setting aside her childish angst about her love life, Leyla prepped herself for the meeting with yet another read through of her frankly stellar resume. They were ostensibly meeting about the Expo, but Tyler never went straightforward when he could get circuitous instead.

"Leyla, you're here."

As scheduled, on time, but that never put paid to his loudly acclaiming her timely arrivals.

"Thanks for meeting with me again." She handed over the Expo folder. "I emailed you this, too, so you can forward it. Everyone was very excited about the partnership proposal, and there's a few ideas in there I think will be fun and advantageous to everyone."

He flipped through, lingering a bit on the projected numbers and early response to the podcast chronicling the effort to get everything underway. She knew from how his eyes tracked over and over that part of the page that he'd noted how a future episode was going to feature their work to get the university involved. A clever little carrot; credit to Austin. Instead of commenting on any of the work she'd presented, he said, "You gave Dr. Lang's info to Jenni Klein."

"The job is a great fit for her. OEP is the precise kind of place she's always hoped to make her career." Not voiced: how he should have known that about Jenni, and that the same wasn't true for her. Certainly if he was going to keep claiming close ties to the grad school cohorts, he should have at least that much of a clue. With only a dozen or so students in each M.S. year and a dozen more overall working towards their Ph.Ds, it didn't seem like such a difficult task to keep them all straight, no matter his other job duties.

Dean Tyler batted the air like her words were little enough to consider. "She was all set to go to Alaska."

"It was settling, not being set. Like OEP would have been settling for me. I was counting on Dunlavy, but now that's off the table, I can find something else to settle for that won't mean withholding a perfect opportunity from a friend."

His look presaged one of those 'I speak to you from the bounty of my experience' lectures, and she was not in the mood.

It was to forestall him as much as anything else that she blurted, "I've been looking elsewhere but I'd rather stay in town. This community is important to me, which I expect you know because of all my work on the Expo. But more important than anything, for me, is for me to do work with regulatory impact. I believe in community education and the potential for trickle-up changes, but if we want to make major strides in the climate and ecosystem crises, we need enforceable top-down solutions. We need integrated agriculture-aquaculture and sustainable food systems that alter current consumption trends. Our economic system needs an overhaul or an upheaval or some kind of revolution to forefront conservation and climate change issues. And all of that work needs to be equitable, of course it does, but you and Dunlavy and OEP all need to learn that me being Black isn't the focus of my career; it's me being a damn good scientist that everyone needs to realize."

Dean Tyler sat back, lips pursed. The way he looked at her, without some of usual layers of bonhomie, was almost disconcerting.

After way too long, he asked, "How do you feel about working in the public sector?"

"That man."

"I know you've been holding back on gossip about him

until I graduate but let me promise you now, I will buy you all the tacos in exchange for you breaking your professional code of conduct."

Sally scoffed, but Leyla could see she was tempted.

"Anyway, it was like that moment at the end of the Willy Wonka movie—the Gene Wilder one."

"Naturally." They both paused and glanced up in memorial to the best Wonka.

"Right, so there I was, feeling like Charlie Bucket giving back an everlasting gobstopper and braced to back away fast in case Dean Tyler starts to leap around and hug me and drag me onto a glass elevator."

"Not without me, you wouldn't."

"Course not. You're the Grandpa Joe in this story."

Leyla didn't know if Derek just so happened to walk by every time Sally busted out laughing, or if he'd taken to lurking in case he could catch her at it, but what she really wanted to observe was Sally being flustered by the intern's attention to every anti-librarian-stereotype her friend embodied.

Either way, it was a needed release of all the tension from her meeting. She'd been sitting there braced the whole time, after day upon day of stress and doom-scrolling every job board in the state, and it turns out all along Dean Tyler knows a guy at the California Coastal Commission looking to contract someone experienced with database construction and analysis and emerging best practices in ocean ecology? And he just didn't bother to mention it because of his set notions.

Yeah, Leyla needed to throw gobstoppers back in the face of would-be puppeteers more often.

"That's the sucky thing," she said, even though she hadn't provided context clue one for Sally to follow her brain's train.

"More words." Sally made a 'why are you staring at us' face at Derek, then turned to her. "Sucky in what way?"

Leyla rolled her eyes at herself so her friend wouldn't have to. "I don't think he'd have ever bothered to bring it up if I hadn't done like Austin and thrown out my usual planned and organized way of speaking to him. All this time, I figured I had to be that way—not just with Tyler, but his communication style is more chaotic than most—because I had to stay on point and focused on the endgame. And here it is, endgame time, and I'm near about to lose, and all I can think of is how Austin does that 'talk until a new idea or a truth comes out' thing. So I tried it, and now I've got this lead, and ..."

She slumped her whole self deeper into the unforgiving chair opposite the library reference desk.

"And if you had the choice, you're wondering if you'd pick Austin instead of a replacement dream job?"

Sally had her in a hug before she'd even finished her nod of defeat.

Chapter Thirty-Four

Austin was done.

First time in ages, he'd cleared his entire project wall. He could have grabbed the opportunity to touch up the paint, except that would somehow mean he was committed to staying on once Cypress Villas took over. Which he definitely was not.

It was all thanks to a bunch of restless days spent knocking out every single maintenance request, including a few projects he'd made up on the spot to stay occupied. The new tenant in 104 had dropped off a goddamn basket of cookies as thanks for helping him move in, when Austin had been the one to jump on the opportunity in his quest to do any and everything with his excessive energy. He'd even updated all his paperwork, mainly so he'd have no need for any in-person conversations with his father.

Once he found himself hinging up the stovetop to sponge under the burners, he knew he'd hit his low. Not because it was a bad chore. But he'd done it like a week after Abraham moved out, and there was no chance it needed doing again.

He packed up every scrubbed clean reusable cup he could

find, along with a set of headphones he'd upgraded past, and took off to Pier Three. Upstairs, he checked every connection in the recording studios to be sure they were tight, and ran a dust mop under the conference table. He posted up fresh signage about the equipment protocols and checked that everyone on the studio schedule had signed the use agreements. He tightened the loose backs on two of the conference chairs.

Now the only useful things he could do involved being close to other humans, so he pulled up his nonexistent socks and slunk into the Pier Three office, managing to shut himself in before anyone spoke to him. He dismissed the flurry of greetings through the door as unimportant.

Instead, he pulled out all the papers and notes and entries he had and created four weeks' worth of shifts, with two more provisional scheduled after that. And no, he didn't forget to bring on extra staff during the Surfside Swell Expo. He wrote a sticky note to that effect and slapped it on the top left corner of the work computer's keyboard.

He always did that, placing it so it covered the A and the W. Didn't know if his siblings ever noticed how he left his important messages to them on top of their joint initials. But it amused him so he kept doing it.

Less amusing: when his brother don't even knock, just barged in wearing his green backpack. "Come on."

"You're not on shift today. What are you doing here?"

"You're not either. Come on." Abe tugged him out like he was child's wagon.

"Did Cleo call and tell you I was here?"

"No."

So it was Ruthie. He shot her a look as they passed, because of course Abraham took him through the cafe instead of out the back. "So, what, you got a message and backed out of some cave and hustled down here to fetch me?"

"I wasn't caving."

First laugh he'd had all day, thanks to deliberately misunderstanding his brother's color coded backpack system.

Abraham seemed to be refusing to be amused. "I was at home. I got the backpack for us."

"Oh, no. No no no." He stopped in the middle of the parking lot. He knew perfectly well what the green bag meant. "You're not making me go hiking."

"You need out of your head."

"That's what surfing is for."

"Yeah, but if we're surfing you won't talk to me."

A damn good point, but he wasn't gonna say so. "Can we at least go fishing, then?" He tried to detour towards the pier with negative amounts of success.

"Stop whining. If we go fishing you'll come up with some excuse to bail the second we cast our lines. I'm keeping you more hostage than that."

"So this is a hostage situation. Abraham, that's illegal or whatever the fuck."

All he got back was an unbothered shrug. Seemed like the law didn't matter in this situation, and also, neither did the past ten or fifteen years of Austin pointing out that he hated hiking. And never mind how much Abraham said it didn't make sense to love surfing and biking only to treat a simple walk in the woods as the heights of horror.

Some snarky part of his brain pointed out that he knew precisely why he hated it: 'cause he was always defining himself in opposition to his brother. Abraham liked caving and hiking, so Austin liked fishing and surfing. He supposed it was a good thing Alicia don't have the same defiant tendencies, since the brothers had land and sea covered. She'd have been left with hot air balloons and skydiving or something.

Apparently that wasn't her way, since she'd been the one to make them all like fancy coffee and practicing yoga and the concept of using their inherited wealth to empower people who hadn't grown up with a safety net. It was the way she was the most classic middle child, finding glue to stick them all together, no matter what elements they preferred to inhabit.

"You ever go parasailing?"

Abe said, "Couple times, yeah, when I was on vacation with Ernesto and his family that time." Ernesto was one of Abe's college roommates. These days he lived in Monterey, selling commercial real estate.

"Hey, does Ernesto know anybody at the aquarium?"

Abraham parked at the trailhead, shouldered that damn green backpack, and set off, forcing Austin to go along with him if he wanted an answer to his question.

Thing was, he needed that answer. Sally'd told him a couple days back that Leyla was looking at jobs at the Monterey Bay Aquarium, and never mind how that dart to his heart was a natural consequence of asking his friend for news. If Leyla was leaving Surfside, it was to pursue her dreams the best way she could, so he needed to help. And the only thing he was good at that she'd ever said wasn't her strength, was making connections.

Maybe he was only now learning how to figure out if those connections were also friends, but finding them to start with? Finding out if they knew someone who knew someone? That, he could do. Not to interrogate them on Leyla's behalf, but to make introductions if it would get her any kind of information or assistance.

It wasn't until they'd veered onto the longer trail that Abraham answered. "I don't know, but probably. You know his cousins are all over that town. I can text him."

"Cool, good. Now?"

His brother stopped his relentless striding deeper into the spider-infested forest to stare him down.

He stared right back, arms crossed. It wasn't like he

couldn't tackle Abraham to the ground and steal his keys. He wasn't even wearing his prosthesis, so Austin wouldn't have to worry about accidentally damaging the thing.

Or he could walk right back to the trailhead and call for a ride, but he let the tackling option sit forefront of his expression.

Abraham rolled his eyes in a super-dramatic way before pulling out his cell and texting. "Happy now?" He continued hiking, and Austin followed.

"Yeah. What about Callie?" She, too, used to live in Monterey, before a fire destroyed her home and much of her work. It had impelled her to move up to Surfside and into apartment 104, throwing her into Abraham's orbit.

"How would I know? Ask her yourself."

He did, glad that at least they weren't so far into nowhere that he'd lost his signal. He even took a pic of Abraham, walking deeper into the towering redwoods, that he thought was sufficiently artsy enough to impress his brother's partner. She didn't needed bribing to answer him, but one of his connections-making tricks was to bring smiles into the conversation. If he wasn't a jerk about it, he tended to get faster responses.

He saved the photo so he could send it to Mom when necessary.

"You're good enough as you are."

Austin stashed his phone and failed to figure out what his brother was talking about. "What?"

"You're a good business partner, too. I'm glad we're co-owners of Pier Three. I've learned shit from you. And all of us together have complementary strengths."

"Fuck, Abraham, you don't have to sound like you're reciting this careful speech from memory. It's not the Oscars."

Abe shouldered him like they were on the best of terms

now he'd gotten his rehearsed statement out there. "Since when do you care about the Oscars?"

"I don't. But I know enough about them to know your speech would just be you saying how Mom has always been your biggest supporter and spending the rest of the time until they played you off swooning over Callie."

Abraham snorted, but didn't counter-argue him. Instead, he went back to his script. "We'll respect you and love you and like hanging out with you even if you quit and follow Leyla to Monterey or wherever. You don't need to prove yourself worthy for us."

Austin scrubbed at his hair. Sighed. Plodded forward on the damn leaf-fall strewn path. "Was dragging me out here to get me 'out of my head' just so you could try to crawl into it instead? You're so fucking off base I don't even know where to start with you."

"So explain it." Abraham rounded on him, spilling words that didn't sound the least rehearsed. "Explain why I'm so wrong. Explain what you thought would happen if I knew you'd gone back to school. You must have hid it from me for months while we were living together. All those times you'd say you were going biking or surfing, and came back with no hint of windburn. Is that when you were going to classes and lying about it? What about when I tried to borrow a legal pad and found your desk locked? Was that because you didn't want there to be any chance I'd see your schoolwork?"

"You broke into my desk?"

He threw up his arm like he was the one who deserved to be exasperated. "No, you suspicious shit. I went to the store and bought my own damn office supplies. But why did I have to? What did you think would happen if I knew you were working on your degree?"

They'd gone far enough. Austin was done.

He tugged one of the water bottles from the side pocket of

the green backpack and sat his ass on the trail. "You're really making this about you right now."

Abe dropped down beside him and glared into the mid-distance. "You hurt my feelings."

Fucking hell. He tried not to respond, he really did.

But every deep breath he tried to take shook and stuck in a shallow hole his chest.

Every time he tried to press his lips closed, they trembled and set his whole jaw to quivering.

And the whole time, his brother was right there at his shoulder, huffing like he deserved for Austin to cut himself deeper open, no matter how much it set his wounds to ooze and ache.

"Fine, okay. So imagine this: we're living together, and yeah, it was years I hid this from you, so feel free to get higher on your self-righteous horse right now. And for all those years, imagine you know I'm working on my degree. And every day you pull your big brother takes care of everyone act. Whether I'm at work or at home, you're there to check if I've done my goddamn homework. If I signed up for the right classes on time for the next semester. If I'm sure I don't need any help understanding the math concepts. In that situation, congrats to you because your feelings are all happily butting in on my life. But what about me? What about how I don't want to have Mr. Two Degrees in Five Years watching my every move, and making me feel more of a failure for every second I'm struggling with stats? Or ever-so-carefully reassuring me that no one thinks I'm a fuckup if I can't even get through community college? What about what I need in this situation? So to hell with you and your hurt feelings. I made the choice to protect myself, and I'm not apologizing for it."

He glared at Abraham, whose face had pinched in on itself so much his lips had disappeared behind the beard.

"Did you know it was a good month after you moved out

before I brought any of my college shit out of my bedroom? Cause what if you walked in someday and saw it? Then I'd have to—to be stuck doing what I'm doing now, and explain why it's not always sunny skies to be your little brother. In case you wondered, I also love you and respect you and like hanging out with you. Though how you could wonder that when I've spent my whole life following you around, I don't know. Probably you don't. Probably you think you're totally worthy of how I've been devoted to you, but guess what? I'm living through all this flux and pain right now, and your instinct is to force me to explain myself to you, so maybe you should stop listening to Mom for a minute and realize you're not as fucking perfect as you think you are."

He swallowed hard and wiped at his stinging eyes. Fucking forest full of mold spores or whatever. There was a log not ten feet away, covered with orange and white mushrooms. He shuddered to think what muck he'd discover if he turned the thing over.

One thing he knew for sure: he'd uncovered more than enough squirming underbellies for the day.

Chapter Thirty-Five

It was a warm day, and the waves beckoned. She hauled Rainbow downstairs and even the tar-tinged air of the parking lot felt like a relief after spending too long creating and verifying her account with the state hiring system, and transferring all her info from her resume and her university accounts, and editing her writing sample, and checking and checking and triple checking she had it all right. Not that she'd hit submit yet, not until she'd checked once more, but she needed away from her computer. From all screens.

From anything that might chime or buzz or otherwise fool her heart into thinking there could be a message from Austin heading her way.

The ocean was the perfect respite. Even if it did keep shooting her back towards shore like it wanted her to face shit she wasn't in the mood for. Joke was on the Pacific, though, cause she just turned Rainbow around every time and paddled back to the lineup, where she could bob on the eternal rise and fall of the lull. Where she could rest her eyes on the horizon or shift them to gauge the direction of approaching swells. Where she could charge at her wave, cut into it and ride it off the lip

—balance and surge and air all on her side, so she was goddamn dancing and flying and her noodle arms didn't matter and her family getting precious about where they'd stay for graduation didn't matter and Chad sure as shit didn't matter. Neither did where she'd have to move, or what her job would be, or whether or not Austin would come back into her life.

All that mattered was her feet gripping Rainbow's deck and her body shifting over the shining green-grey water and her heart soaring as she flew into a kick out and turned around to go back for more.

Abraham drove him home. Before he got out of the car, his brother held out his keyring. "Take your key back. I should have returned it when Callie and I got our place."

Austin could refuse. Mention it made sense for someone to have a spare. Ask that his brother just knock next time before letting himself in.

Instead, he dug his thumbnail in to divide the ring and unspool his key.

While he did, Abe said, "I'm sorry."

It was all he said, no further exploration of how Abraham had let their years of big brother-little brother dynamics strike a blow against their adult siblings-as-friends dynamic. A dynamic which Austin had thought they'd solidified.

To be a little fair, Austin also wasn't apologizing for sliding awry of that shift. His brother wasn't the only one who'd fucked things up there.

He initiated a hug before leaving the car. And instead of going straight to his place, he climbed to the top floor and knocked on his parents' door.

He didn't preamble, just launched in with what was on his

mind. "I was acting like your kid, instead of like your employee."

Dad led him into the kitchen and handed him a beer. "You're both. You can't separate them."

The hell he couldn't. Or at least, he could try, especially now he was jettisoning one of those roles. He didn't contradict his father, though. "I haven't come by to say I've changed my mind, or to be talked into anything. That's the first thing. But second is, thanks for trusting me with this job—of training me for it in the first place, you and Val. I've liked it. But I won't keep doing once you sell."

Mom wandered in then, acting casual like she'd had no idea he was in the place, even though he'd grown up in their penthouse and knew perfectly well how sound carried in it.

He kept his focus on Dad. "You should have told me what you were doing, looking for management companies. Negotiating the sale. Not cause I'm your employee, but cause I'm your kid. You should have said you changed your mind about me taking over someday. Even if it was awkward, even though it means telling me I'm not good enough and you like it better when that goes unsaid. You still should have faced up to saying it."

Dad nearly lunged to grasp his hands. "Austin, honey."

"No, Simon, he's right. We should have confronted him."

Fucking hell.

"Katherine."

He wrenched loose a hand and held it up. "Say what you need, Mom."

"I think what you're really here to ask is if I'm the one who talked Dad into selling, or if it's both of us thinking all those things you've decided are our true opinion of you."

He crossed his arms and remembered all the times he'd done that already that day, and the way Leyla called out the move as part of his insecure neediness. So, instead, he picked at the beer label.

"We love you, Austin."

He did not roll his eyes, because he loved and respected his parents. But it was a close call. "Love you too, Mom."

"But you have to stop acting like we ruined your life. Or like we rule it. Being the building super is just a job. You're good at it; the tenants often say nice things and I'm not even sure they all know you're our son. But it's not who you are, it's not your identity. If you stay here once we sell, or if you go, it's not a fuck you to us."

"Katherine."

"Mom."

She rolled her eyes at both of them. "He's an adult. You are an adult, Austin. You're your own man and I don't know where you came up with this fixed idea about how we don't believe you can take care of yourself, but you made a big deal about that when we had brunch. So put this on your record: I know, and Dad knows, that you can take care of yourself just fine. We didn't ask Cypress Villas to keep you on because we need someone to pity you. We asked because we knew this change was coming out of the blue for you and wanted you to have as long as you needed to make other plans. If other plans are what you want to make."

"Why did you do it that way, though? Make all these arrangements and not let me in until the end?" He had other questions, but that was the one that burbled to the top of the pile.

Dad cleared his throat. "That was me."

He downed his beer and waited for more.

"When you were a kid, always so fascinated by Val's work and paying attention to everything to do with the building ... It's a parent thing, I think. Imagining how every little thing about your kids will play out when they're older."

"I used to think Alicia would be a dentist because when she was nursing she loved to stick her fingers in my mouth," Mom put in.

"She did, didn't she?" Dad chuffed a little. "Anyhow, you were our little fix-it guy, and maybe it was your ADHD that made me go in hard on imagining you taking over the building one day. Maybe it was me feeling a little protective of you. But, Austin, that was when you were a kid. I didn't think—maybe I should have, but I didn't think you'd still be holding on to that more than a dozen years later."

"Back then we also didn't think a lot about what we'd want when we reached this age." Mom shrugged. "We maybe assumed at least one of the three of you would be interested in this place, but we also assumed we'd still like it as a business to hand down."

He started back a bit. "Wait, you don't like the building anymore?"

Dad patted soothingly at the kitchen table like it was an extension of the entire structure. "We do. Sometimes less, sometimes more, but it's home. It's where you three grew up. It's also pretty demanding. And we're not saying you couldn't manage it. You could."

Austin narrowed his eyes at this further mixing of their message.

"Dad doesn't mean you should, though. When you opened Pier Three, that's when we saw you engaged with your passion. We're so impressed with everything you've done with it—all of you, of course, and we love that you're building it together. But you in particular have found ways to use all your skills there. Construction and working with people and making an environment that brings customers back. Seeing that? Austin. You got it so completely backwards when you accused us of thinking you were an albatross to convey with the complex. It's so clear to us that the building is the albatross, and more than anything we want you free to soar away from it."

"When you're ready," Dad put in.

"Right. When you're ready, and if that's your choice, you should fly."

AUSTIN: if you want and if you have time, can we meet?

AUSTIN: if not, I understand

AUSTIN: I have something for you, this is on top of the talking I want to do, but I can email it if you don't want to see me

AUSTIN: I can meet any time that works for you. People said they would cover my shifts. And now I'll stop texting and wait for an answer but if you don't answer in two days I'll email but it will just be the list for you and nothing emotional or personal you have to mess with, thanks

Must be years of experience plus also his wider handspan that let him text so much in rapid succession. Leyla smoothed her own hand over her brow and neck and heart like she could settle down all the internal responses with a little external touch. It worked, sorta. Except then she'd thought about touch and about Austin's wide hands and all that set off a whole other slew of internal responses.

She missed touch.

Specifically, she missed Austin's touch.

She wanted to text him right back. Or call. Or fling herself into the library to make Sally deep-dive into it all. Or screen-shot it for Zora's dissection. Or just know already what would happen when they met, so she wouldn't have so many competing ideas bounding through her mind.

But she was a scientist, so she looked at the available data and drew conclusions. It was bound to be some kind of make-up or apology, because he'd hardly go asking Ruthie or his brother or whoever to cover his shift just so they could fight more. Or to certify a break-up. Plus, he wanted to give her something, which wasn't the norm for calling it quits with someone. Not if the something given could be emailed without her getting emotional. Maybe it was him getting emotional he worried about?

Fuckity fuck fuck. She wasn't going to flowchart her reply.

Leyla: Tomorrow at 2?

Austin: perfect, yea - at Pier3? Your place? Or mine? I can make you lunch.

Leyla: I'll come to you, no lunch needed, but latte welcome

Austin: it's a date

Austin: crap, sorry

Austin: it's no pressure, and I'll see you then.

Ridiculous to have missed his stream of consciousness texts, too. She threw herself into incorporating the final notes and edits from her Research Mentor on the defendable version of her capstone paper. She marked a couple of areas where she might play with the text on her slides, because they were still too numbers-and-words heavy. And now she had her Readers' approval on the paper, she had to zero in on the presentation.

Quinn's graphics were genius, which helped.

Even if admiring them was yet another chance for thoughts of Austin to slip in and mess with her concentration.

Leyla: How about you bring me that latte now?

Austin: Yeah? Yeah! You're at your place? Twenty minutes?

She had a few weeks before the presentation, after all. And since this wasn't a break-up visit—she was nearly positive—it would be less distracting to have it over and done with.

Even if twenty minutes was a scant amount of time to hustle around and scoop laundry into a basket and wash her study-grit-filled eyes and apply a layer of lipgloss.

Twenty-five, and she'd also fluffed the couch cushions and texted her roommates there might be an overnight guest.

At twenty-seven, she wondered how to retract a text.

Twenty-eight, she gave up googling for an answer.

Finally, twenty-nine minutes later—she knew because she kept looking at his text like he might be recanting or updating or anything that would give her nerves a direction to take—he knocked.

"Oh. You're wet."

His eyes when he was soaked, and she'd noticed this in the ocean before, turned luminous and huge. They caught at every scrap of her attention, so she had full awareness of all the emotions he displayed.

Happiness. Trepidation. Eagerness. Nerves.

"It's raining."

"Is it?" She backed to let him in and finally glanced at the window. It was a proper downpour, which was unusual for their coastal area. "Do you need a towel?"

"No, just a trashcan." He lifted an umbrella. "I grabbed this when I went to the cafe for your latte. I don't think whoever abandoned it for our lost and found will come looking for it."

He handed over her drink, and she took in more and more about him. The more-formal-than-usual clothes, which were drenched only on the right shoulder and back. The fresh shave and raw shadows under his eyes. The bulky backpack he set beside the sofa before toeing off his shoes.

"Where were you when I texted?"

"Coming back from class. I ..." He cleared his throat and shed his jacket, lifting the hem of his shirt to swipe at the raindrops on his face. "I gave my talk today, the one about data collection bias? Glad that's over."

"How'd it go?" Because despite his wry voice, she wasn't going to fall into the traps he liked to set about denigrating his academic pursuits.

He nodded. "Good, I think. Not terrible, anyway, which it might have been without your help. I'm passing everything this semester."

"Which you did last semester, too, and no one was helping you."

He plunked down on the sofa, then leapt up. "Sorry. I forgot to say sorry for being late."

"It was raining and you stopped to get me this drink. I think you get a pass." Even if she'd had a few minutes there of wondering if he'd run off to hide from her again.

"Still. Sorry." He crossed his arms and blushed and uncrossed them and sat again, fingers beating out a pattern across his thighs. "Did you want to sit? Did you want me to sit?"

She took the opposite end of the couch. He leaned forward to rummage in his backpack, retrieving an orange file folder.

"What's this?" It held three pages of names and emails and notes on each. "'Ernesto's cousin; maintains the watercraft at MBA,'" she read out. "Do I know who Ernesto is? And why does it matter what his cousin Carlos does?"

"Yeah, no. You probably don't. But that's everyone I could find with any kind of connection to the Monterey Bay Aquarium." He glanced down at his tap-tap-tapping fingers. "Ernesto and Abraham were college roommates."

She cleared her throat. "Austin."

"And like I said, you don't need my help. I'm not saying I'm any use for your career, how could I be? But once you're there, maybe one or two of these people will be good to know. Lay of the land, or, you know, best coffee shop in the area, or—"

This man. "Austin."

He rushed on despite her interruption. "And I didn't tell anyone we were dating. Are dating? Once dated? I didn't, I mean. There won't be awkward questions."

Finally, he hushed up. Regarded her with those brown eyes and flushed cheeks and hair every which way and chest heaving like he was still running from the car in the rain.

She handed back the folder. "I'm not going to need this."

Chapter Thirty-Seven

"No, right. Of course." Austin regretted refusing the towel now. He could have used any kind of shield.

She shifted to face him, crossed legs and pink-red lips and one of her perfect shoulders just daring to peep out from her collar like he needed another distraction or any more memories of the soft skin he'd once had the unholy pleasure of kissing. "I'm not applying for an aquarium job."

His throat filled with static and foam and at least forty-five distinct grains of sand. He managed to say, "Alaska?"

She laughed. "Do you think me and Jenni are interchangeable? I thought only Dean Tyler had those misconceptions. We didn't trade jobs."

"Right, that makes sense."

Her casual posture and smiling eyes and the fact she hadn't thrown him out—it all made him happier than he'd been since some foggy day before he'd fucked up his life.

"I missed you."

Leyla's smile didn't quite disappear, but he knew he hadn't said the right thing. He should have typed it up when he was making the connections list.

Instead, he'd done something silly and immature and hardly befitting how deep his feelings for her were. And the hell of it was, he'd trapped himself. It was either go through with his plan, or mess up the apology he'd finally nerved himself to make. And he couldn't, could *not*, run away again.

So he pulled the other thing he'd prepared out of his backpack.

He handed her a square box. "It had my new headphones. It's not apology technology. Did I say sorry yet?"

She took the box, shaking her head. "You also jumped right past finding out about my job."

Austin thunked his head against the sofa back. "I did. Sorry for that, too. I want to hear. If you want to tell me. I'm mixing this whole thing up."

His legs were braced like he would stand again, so she scooted close enough to brush his thigh with her knee. "I'm going to open this now."

He groaned. "You deserve so much better than this."

"True."

They both laughed, and it sank them a touch closer together. Her whole body lit up and let go at the same time. It was like a circuit completed: she didn't have to hold all of her tension within herself anymore, and the pure damn relief of energy flowing freely between them let her relax like she hadn't in days.

"Leyla. Hi."

"Hi."

"I want to know why you aren't going to Monterey and why Sally tormented me by claiming you were. I want to know what your Readers said about your final draft. I want to know the whole string of insults your sister laid against me."

Damn him and his breathtaking amounts of intensity. "The box?"

"You're beautiful."

She huffed out a breath, because being around him sometimes was like being caught in the impact zone between the shoreline and the breaking waves, and all the turtle rolls in the world weren't getting her back to the lineup. "Stop derailing me."

His crooked canine flashed before he pressed his lips closed and mimed zipping them.

She opened the box and a tumbling jumble of folded sticky notes scattered across her lap. Yellow and neon green and orange and pink and neon pink and blue. Frogs, hearts, boats. More hearts. Butterflies in every shade.

He plucked a pink flower from the valley between their legs and handed it over. "Open it?"

Even folded, she could read some of his scrawl. "'I teach everyone how to make a hazelnut latte on the first day of their barista training.'" She smoothed the folds. "You do?"

"In case I'm not around when you come in. I don't want you disappointed."

She tried a frog. "I am responsible for myself and my feelings."

A blue butterfly. "I love you."

An orange fish of some kind. "You deserve space to experience your sadness and your joy and everything in between, and I should have given that to you."

Yellow heart: "I made Noah promise to alert me every time you came to bonfire so I could practice saying stuff to you before I got there even though half the time I couldn't say them."

Pink butterfly: "I love you."

Neon green butterfly: "I love you."

Neon green flower: "The way your mind works is a

miracle of precision and knowledge and generosity towards the world and I'm awed by it."

Neon pink boat: "I made you feel like I wasn't dedicated to you and to our relationship and that's one of the crappiest things I've done."

Every colorful butterfly proclaimed his love. Everything else was a mix of praise, confessions about the ways he orbited her long before she was aware of it, and mea culpas regarding their fight on the Friday of Doom.

He found another butterfly on the floor and handed it to her.

She cupped it in her palm. "I already know what this one says." Indeed, the entire message spanned the wings without her unfolding it.

"But it bears repeating. And, Leyla, listen. I'm not expecting anything in return, okay, that's the main thing. I don't think you opened that one yet." He combed through the origami shapes, and the way his fingers skittered over her lap was unbearable and she wanted more. Ignoring what had to be practically visible longing on her part, he came up with flowers of a few different hues, scanning and rejecting one before opening another. "Here you are: 'Even if I comprehend and apologize for every way I fucked up, I understand you're under no obligation to take me back.'"

His voice had gotten thready at the end, and he looked away from her. Without regard to if she'd opened them or not, he scooped notes back into the box.

She put a hand over his. "Don't take them away from me. Don't take ..." She bit her cheek to halt her words, because she was overwhelmed and it made her want to blurt out any kind of thing instead of being sure her response was the best option for her.

For her life, for her heart, for her future.

For their future.

She took a beat. Came up with a different way to keep him talking while she let herself settle into processing. "How long did you spend making these?"

"I don't know really. It wasn't all at once." He shrugged, which was only a wisp of motion in the places they were touching, but each of those brushed nerves flew hither and yon like wildfire through her body.

"Every time I thought of something else to say to you, I wrote it down and stuck it on the wall. I had this idea I could do like you do, and organize all my scattered comments into, like, a thesis? But then I thought about how you don't expect me to change how I express myself. You never ask me to change the way I think or the way I work, or told me I was wrong for how I get stuff done. Plus, I couldn't figure out how to say everything all at once, which is what I wanted. So then I thought that if I give you all the words at once, you'd ..." He trailed off and shook his head.

She squeezed his hand and brought their bodies closer. "You gave me a bright colorful explosion of everything you wanted to say to me and trusted me to understand."

His eyes screwed shut for a moment, but then he opened them and let her see all the depths he brought to her. "One of the notes, I'm pretty sure, says something about not making you do the mental and emotional work of carrying our relationship. And I hope that's not what I'm doing. Hell, I hope there's a relationship here at all, never mind one I'm learning to be good enough for."

"I don't like that."

He sucked in air. Blew it out. "Which part?"

Never mind her processing time. Never mind crushing all his beautiful paper thought-explosions. Never mind the rest of the explanations and dissections and negotiations. She straddled him and raked her fingers into his damp-soft hair and kissed the ever-loving fuck out of Austin Octavio Wells.

Chapter Thirty-Eight

"I don't like." She kissed his lips. His jaw.

He palmed her waist.

She nuzzled his neck, nip after nip under his ear. "When you doubt."

His hands were spasms of need.

"Yourself."

Whatever she was saying dissolved in a mist of need and relief and also tears? Because he was crying? But she kissed his tears, and it was nothing he'd ever experienced before and it was the most real and more meaningful and most overwhelming moment of his life?

He surged up, holding her torso to his, and they stumbled and kissed and touched and walked down the hall to her room. "Is this okay?"

She tugged up the hem of his shirt and he fumbled open the buttons until they'd maneuvered it off him and onto the floor. And then she shimmied out of her shorts and he was so damn parched for her.

"Leyla."

"Austin." Her smile filled his lungs and fizzled through his veins. So, yeah, fuck restraint and all they'd talk through later: he knelt and she sat and all the things they did, their hands roaming and legs spreading and throats groaning, all of it was the two of them as one. They were a unity of movement, of heightening desire, of pleasure and of loving and of love.

When she'd come and his tongue was coated with her taste and he wore her scent on his face, Leyla flopped back on her bed and scratched at his skull until he managed to prop his forearms on the mattress and regard her.

"Hey there, Dawn Patrol."

He laughed, but he was sure he was blushing, too. Why, he didn't know, but he'd given up on expecting himself to make sense around Leyla. He never had, and she'd still given him another chance, and he'd decided to stop his habit of running away from anything he feared was going to bind him down.

"Hi. I love you."

"Yeah? I hadn't noticed." She scooped a paper butterfly from her bra and waggled it at him. "You shouldn't be so subtle next time."

He flashed her a smile and crawled his way onto the bed beside her.

She tipped her chin at him. "You're not naked enough."

"That, I can fix." He shucked his jeans and contorted to get at his socks.

"Wait."

Austin froze, which wasn't easy but he'd done lots of boat pose in yoga practice, so he did his best. "Yeah?"

"What are you wearing?"

He sank back and looked at her. "Boxers and one sock?"

She poked at his side. "Hilarious. Explain why your boxers are boring now?"

He blushed down to his damn nipples. "I ... yeah. I bought new ones."

"You did? Why?" Leyla propped herself on one elbow.

Her eyes did that thing where they were magnets and he had no ability, or desire, to resist her pull. But she gently pushed him back after a not-gentle kiss.

"It's not what you said about me doubting myself. At least, I don't think so. But I'm realizing that a lot of how I think about myself is centered on what my family thinks of me, you know? Of course you know. And it's not just how I mainly value the things about myself that're useful to them, because another part of it is how I'm the family clown. The one everyone can laugh around. Or at. This is a fucking odd conversation to have when I can't stop staring at your breasts."

"Mm-hmm."

He closed his eyes. "Yeah, exactly. It's such a crap habit. No matter what, never mind my erection or anything, because here comes another joke. I decided restocking my underwear drawer was a good place to start."

He didn't open his eyes, which wasn't the same as running away and hiding. Not quite.

It did mean he was startled when Leyla wrapped her hand around his cock and pumped. He lifted his ass when she lowered the basic blue boxers, and next he got to watch her remove her top and bra. His one sock was the only thing stopping them from being entirely naked together.

"I'm getting a job with the California Coastal Commission. I'll be based out of Surfside. It's contract work, but they encouraged me get my application in because they expect a full-time position to open by the end of the year."

Never mind his erection, Austin's whole self was vibrating with excitement. He tackle-hugged her. "Leyla, that's amazing. I mean, I hope it's amazing. I hope it's all the right things for you, for your career."

"Oh, it is. So far seems so, anyway. And you know how I got it?"

"I mean, from being spectacular, right?"

Her kisses were butterflies, more vibrant and more vital than the paper creatures he'd given her. She settled them so he covered her, and all his skin warmed and relaxed because it rested against all her skin. "Nope. I was spectacular all along, but that damn gatekeeper wasn't doing a damn thing for me. Nor were my independent searches, but my point here's about this job. I was in there talking to Dean Tyler and he knows everything on my resume, right? We'd talked about all of it. But he was still trying to pin me in all these roles to do with me being Black instead of me being, as you say, spectacular at the science. So instead of letting him talk at me again, some more, about the importance of equity or whatever that yes, is important, but—"

"It's not saving the oceans with smart policies that held corporate and government entities to account."

She bit his shoulder, which made him nuzzle hers, but he wanted to hear the rest.

He touched his forehead to hers and asked, "What did you do?"

"I thought about how you speak from the heart, from the soul, instead of measuring all your words first. I channeled your approach and told him the clear facts of how he wasn't working with the right ideas about me. And then that ass was like, 'oh in that case here's a perfect job exactly tailored to all the things you're saying.'"

He shook his head a little. Squeezed in his knees to share his goosebumps with her powerful thighs. "Spectacular, like I said. You embraced the confidence of a mediocre white man to get what you deserve."

Leyla flipped them to straddle above him. "One, I know you're clowning so I'm gonna let you get away with that."

He ran his hands up her ribcage and cupped the swells of her breasts.

"Two. That's nice … Two. I do fucking deserve it."

He lavished attention on her breasts, suckling her nipples into tight brown points.

"Mmm." She leaned away just long enough to grab supplies, and perched so he could finger lube along her entrance and thumb circles on her clit as she sheathed his hard-as-hell erection. "Three."

He swallowed, because Leyla's voice had gone soft and it captured every iota of his attention. "Three?"

She sank down, taking his entire length in one long, perfect slide. "Three. Don't ever, ever again call the man I love 'mediocre.'"

He bucked and thrust and cried, tears obscuring his vision. But Leyla was right there, kissing them away as she bore down on him. They were a damp and sweaty and weeping mess and each drop fused them closer. He'd never in his life been more completely part of someone else. Leyla's hand holding his to her core, her mouth delving into him as a sensual echo of the way he filled her with each grinding, surging thrust.

Again and again they slammed into each other, voices a babble of love and names and moans and yes. Again and again her heat and her muscles clamped around his throbbing cock. He pressed both thumbs along the wall of her clit, pinching inexorably while he sucked her nipple and dug his fingers into her hips. Leyla keened, the spasms starting deep in her core wrapping him into bliss that overpowered his restraint. Spine tingling, balls tight, drenched and delirious with happiness, he joined her in orgasm and ecstasy and love.

"Unggh."

He breathed hard, sprawled half-below her. "Mm."

It took a few, but she figured out how to speak words again. "Austin?"

"Mmm?"

Shifting so she could flop on the pillow and look at him, she said, "One thing."

"Aren't you up to four things now?"

Took too much energy to bap his chest, so she just flapped her wrist once. "You're cute."

Then something struck her and she sat up to glare at him. "And also by the way: you are funny. I love how funny you are. I don't know how to be funny like that. You don't gotta perform for me, but I'm telling you, how you make me laugh is one of my favorite things. My best people—that's Sally and Zora and you, if you're keeping count—are ones who make me laugh."

Austin slid the sheets down and tucked them both to lean against the headboard. "I'm one of your best people?"

"Hell, yes, were you not paying attention when I said I loved you?" She bit her lips to stop from grinning so hard her cheeks hurt.

"I was. I was just fishing for you to tell me again. Excuse me for being shameless."

"Maybe." They were such a mess, but kissing him was still like a sunny day with an offshore breeze. "Back to my fourth thing."

"Fifth. You forgot to count how I make you laugh. Which, since we're counting all these things, your wit is one of the things I love about you. Go look through all those frogs; I'm sure I wrote that down."

Overcome with a fit of self-consciousness, she ducked her head to his shoulder. He kissed her crown and nuzzled at her hair in a way she'd fuss about if he hadn't had her thrashing all over the covers not half an hour back. "I've spent a lot of years focused on just this."

He bumped his hip to hers. "This?"

She laughed. Of course. "No, silly. My degrees, my career. Going back to when I first learned to surf and decided I wanted to work on the ocean someday. It's been nothing but making schedules and researching plans and following them for … for so long, Austin."

"I know."

"But you don't. I mean, you do, because I told you and you listened, but it's how I've defined myself for a decade or more now. It never stopped you from seeing other parts of me, the me that's not all about school and work. I'm grateful for that."

"Hey, Leyla." He cradled her face and smoothed away the frown in her brow. "You shine. Everything about you. The way you zero in on your goals and make them happen, that's amazing and one of the things I love about you—I know that's on a note. Or two. Or three. And I'm not going to put up a fight about it because I'm too grateful that you love me, but I still can't understand how you think I'm good enough for someone as brilliant and driven as you."

"That's the thing." She pulled away so she could full-arm point at him. "You're wrong about the good enough thing, but never mind that. I'm talking about how you've been doing all this reevaluating of your own self-conception and separating out what's important from what's holding you back, and that's what I need to do. In just a few weeks I'm presenting my capstone, and then I'm graduating, and I have to figure out what I'm like when I'm not focused on some goal on a project sheet."

He drew her fingers to his lips for a kiss. "I've only done any evaluating because I had to figure out why you don't think the same things about me as my family thinks. Or that I think. Thought. And thought that my family thought, 'cause I was wrong about a lot of that, but never mind that, as you say."

Austin snuggled back into her side. "If I can figure out some new truths about myself, you sure as hell can come up with ways to live without a spreadsheet goal. Or make a new one, if that makes you happier."

Their interlaced fingers and intertwined arms and in sync breaths all seemed to suggest that he was right. That she'd figure it out. "Oh, also, I have to move."

"Mmm?"

"That's the fourth thing."

"You might be up to the sixth thing now."

She squeezed his hand. "Whichever it is. Graduation's coming, so I'll need to move off campus. The CCC offices are down past Pier One, but—"

"We can look there. Lots of cute little houses walking distance to Lucille's, I noticed."

Leyla shifted the tension out of her jaw. "I ... was going to suggest your apartment."

"Nah. I'm leaving there. It's all arranged. That's why I know about the cute little houses. I mean, we can look anywhere you want, as long as there's enough room for Rainbow and my quiver. And the twin fin longboard Noah's holding for me to give you at graduation."

Her whole face and maybe her whole body were flowing over with smiles. "Austin, really? You did?"

He bit his lip. "I'm terrible at surprises. I can't ever wait."

Reaching over, she smoothed his lip free, then took it between her own lips in a soul-settling, sexy, sated and sweet kiss. "As long as you can't wait for us to make a life together, you can ruin every surprise you think up forever."

Epilogue

The Expo was so far beyond full swing it was turning into some kind of perpetual motion machine.

Austin never put down his phone, because if he tried it would automatically blare at him that Elmer or Cleo needed more supplies over at their tent on Main Street, or Alicia or Mateo needing him to go repair someone's booth. He knew he looked a ridiculous frazzled mess when Leyla and her parents stopped by Pier Three. The sight of them made him jump, even though he'd been expecting them.

Her folks had decided—against Leyla's protests that it would be boring for them—to come in for her capstone presentation, and stay for the Surfside Swell Expo that weekend.

The capstone had been utterly engaging and not the least boring, in his fascinated opinion, which her parents shared. She'd giggled when he'd confessed his anxieties over them liking him, saying, "To hear everyone else talk about it, you spend every second we're not together talking about how phenomenal I am."

"Well, you are."

"Granted." And, oh, her smile.

It turned out she was right about her parents, as about so much else: his obvious devotion to Leyla was enough to win them over. Almost as easy as it'd been for Leyla to win over his folks, especially since he fessed up to them about his AA degree the day they'd invited all their kids and kids' partners to their 'farewell to the penthouse' dinner. Never mind that he'd enrolled three semesters before he and Leyla started dating; Mom and Dad threw all their happiness over it into a big bucket of joy that encompassed them both.

He rounded the corner after nodding to Ruthie to comp whatever drinks the Robinsons wanted. "Hey, how's your morning been?"

She ruffled his hair into place and he stood there practically levitating with happiness at her touch. He was so gone in love with her. And she didn't act one bit like she minded, tugging him towards the office so they could get in a few proper kisses.

"They love the place."

"Yeah?" He grinned. "What about the balcony, did you tell them I'm going to replace that rail?"

"Yes, relax. We all have faith in your handiness."

They'd found a small fixer-upper house a few minutes from Pier One, and were set to move in at the end of the month. He'd also started working a few contract handyman jobs to keep him busy when he wasn't surfing, studying, making coffee, or worshiping Leyla.

Well, he was always busy worshipping Leyla, but sometimes he multi-tasked and got other stuff done, too.

She'd given him the idea to make videos of some of his projects, and his channel was taking off. He still laughed at having joined the ranks of home repair YouTube dad types, but he had the expertise and it brought him joy, so why not? It was one more way he was using his soon-to-be degree.

Leyla, meanwhile, was set to use hers to save the oceans, starting with the California coast and expanding out from there, if he had his guess.

"You ever think about how you're kind of a superhero?" He pressed his lips together in an attempt to keep hold of her taste, even though they were walking back to the patio where her parents sat.

"Damn you're good for my ego."

"No, but really. You fly on Rainbow."

"And Sparkle."

He hoped like hell no one ever made the connection between her surfboard names and the My Little Pony boxers she'd insisted stay on rotation in his collection. "And on Sparkle. And you vanquished your enemies. And you've got a mighty brain. And you have a mission to save the planet, and you're courageous and focused. I'm pretty sure those are all the qualities."

Leyla drew them to a halt, right there in the middle of Pier Three Coffee, bustling with people on a sunny late spring day, all the buzz of the Surfside Swell Expo in the air. "Austin Wells, you slay me."

"No I don't. You're invincible, we just established that."

The way she looked at him then, it wouldn't take much to convince him that she'd contrived to share her invincibility with him. He felt like he could take on anything in the world, if doing so gave him a chance to be regarded so favorably by Leyla Robinson, certified genius and superhero.

"Guess what Sally told my parents when we ran into her at the university's booth?"

He raised his eyebrows. "Considering she told you not to get involved with Expo in the first place, I sure hope she's enjoying her time on Main Street."

"She was, until I pointed out Derek strolling her way."

"You did? Was he?"

"No, but I had to shut her up somehow. She'd just gone and told Mom and Dad I'm going to marry you someday."

One little flicker of 'is this okay?' lurked in her eyes, and he wasn't having that. Not when she was a thousand percent of his happiness. Plus, the very idea meant his widest and wickedest grin spread all across his face. He wrapped her up and spun her in a circle, and kissed her hard, never mind anyone watching.

"Fuck yeah you are. And, Leyla? It's going to be the best day of my life. I can't wait."

Thanks for riding the swells to happily ever after with Latte for Leyla. Reviews are an invaluable tool for authors, and I'd love to get your honest review at any of the following places, or others of your choosing:

*Stores * Goodreads * Bookbub*

For a complete book list and more, keep scrolling.
Thanks for reading!
-Melanie

<h1 style="text-align:center">Acknowledgments</h1>

I'm verklempt! The Pier Three Coffee series caught my imagination one evening years ago, and I've loved living in the Surfside of my mind throughout the writing process. Leyla was the first partner I thought of for my trio of coffee shop owning siblings, and she's been my on-page companion for the whole series. I hope you all enjoyed spending time with her as much as I have.

I'm grateful for my sensitivity reader and guidance from Salt & Sage Books. No outsider perspective can be without issues, but I appreciate the chance to get closer to good representation.

Thanks to my reader Nancy for naming Rainbow. And thanks to all of my advanced readers for their early feedback. (Click here if you'd like to join the Greene Team to become one of my ARC readers.)

As always, Robert has been the best of husbands, the best 'it's just fine to live and work with you all day every day during a years-long pandemic' partner, and best at advising and editing.

Our sons David and Kieran inspire us and awe us as they move so brilliantly into adulthood, and I'm always touched by their support of my writing career.

Thank you always to my online writing communities, especially my fellow CRW members and my #notwriting and Inclusive Romance Project peers (and the IRP member writing playlist, which got me through many an editing session.) Sophia, you are the best accountability partner ever!

About the Author

Melanie Greene lives in a tiny woodland cottage in a big skyscraper city, with her husband and kids and pets and plants and all the people inhabiting her imagination.

For more info, visit her at www.melaniegreene.com, where you can sign up for her newsletter to access new releases and bonus content.

facebook.com/MelGreeneBooks

twitter.com/Daki_MelGreene

instagram.com/melaniegreeneauthor

www.ingramcontent.com/pod-product-compliance
Lightning Source LLC
Chambersburg PA
CBHW071147180726

48291CB00007B/2361